GRAND CENTRAL
PUBLISHING

LARGE
PRINT

The Hamish Macbeth Series

Death *of a* Green-Eyed Monster

A Hamish Macbeth Murder Mystery

M. C. BEATON
with R. W. Green

GRAND CENTRAL
PUBLISHING

LARGE PRINT

Grand Central Publishing
Hachette Book Group
1290 Avenue of the Americas, New York, NY 10104
grandcentralpublishing.com
twitter.com/grandcentralpub

First U.S. Edition: February 2022

Grand Central Publishing is a division of Hachette Book Group, Inc. The Grand Central Publishing name and logo is a trademark of Hachette Book Group, Inc.

The publisher is not responsible for websites (or their content) that are not owned by the publisher.

The Hachette Speakers Bureau provides a wide range of authors for speaking events. To find out more, go to www.hachettespeakersbureau.com or call (866) 376-6591.

Library of Congress Control Number: 2021947512

ISBNs: 978-1-5387-4670-7 (hardcover), 978-1-5387-4671-4 (large type), 978-1-5387-4672-1 (ebook)

Printed in the United States of America

LSC-C

Printing 1, 2021

Foreword by R. W. Green

Murder is Hamish Macbeth's business. Tracking down fiendish killers is what he does best. Figuring out whether his murder suspects have the ability, opportunity, and motive to perpetrate the crime and then slapping the cuffs on them is his stock-in-trade . . . yet it really shouldn't be, should it?

A police officer based where Hamish lives wouldn't have much experience of murder at all. Hamish's patch of Sutherland is the northernmost part of the Scottish mainland, one of the most sparsely populated regions in the whole of the UK. If you were considering taking a trip to this beautiful, dramatically scenic area, and I recommend that you do, then you needn't be quite as concerned for your safety as reading a Hamish Macbeth murder story might make you believe. Sutherland has a very low crime rate. Of the sixty or so murders committed in Scotland every year, the country's two largest cities—Glasgow and Edinburgh—account for around half, while there is generally only one anywhere near Hamish's territory. A rural police officer like Hamish, therefore, wouldn't get involved in many murder cases. M. C. Beaton knew all that when she first created Hamish—and that's what makes him so special. Sergeant Macbeth is not an ordinary country cop.

M. C. Beaton—Marion—had worked as a crime reporter on the *Scottish Daily Express* in Glasgow, so she knew all about the murky, seedy, violent nature of Scotland's underworld. Judging by the hair-raising stories she liked to tell, she also knew, quite literally, where some of the bodies were buried. That's one of the reasons why she wanted to make Hamish Macbeth different. She didn't want to write about how a real detective operated. She didn't want to write true crime. She had done that. She wanted to provide her readers with some gentle escapism for a rainy afternoon read, set in a landscape that would fire their imaginations. She wanted to give them a hero with endearing contradictions—a hard worker who is prone to skiving off when the mood takes him; a law-abiding police officer who might poach a few salmon or a deer from time to time; an honest cop who deals with people fairly but is also capable of bribing witnesses or planting evidence to get his man. In short, Marion wanted Hamish to be a typically lovable rogue, a maverick with a heart of gold.

The characters he deals with on a regular basis in his fictional home village of Lochdubh are, like the setting itself, inspired in part by the time Marion spent living in a croft in Sutherland and the people she met there. Events in the books are also often based loosely on her real-life experiences in the Highlands. In the very first Hamish Macbeth adventure, *Death of a Gossip*, the story is set in a Highland fishing school, where a group of budding anglers spend a holiday learning how to catch salmon or trout, just as Marion herself had once done. She invented a fictional bubble in which Hamish could exist, but it wasn't entirely watertight—reality regularly leaked in.

I had the enormous pleasure of learning about Hamish not only from the pages of Marion's books but from the master storyteller herself. We first met many years ago in London and, although we didn't meet very often, both being exiled Scots, both having worked on newspapers and magazines, both being writers, we were never stuck for something to talk about. I loved hearing her stories about the different places she had lived around the world, but, more often than not, the conversation would drift back home to Scotland. I had spent time travelling and hill walking in Sutherland, so we were able to compare notes and swap stories about the area.

Then, when she fell ill and was worrying about her writing commitments, I was delighted to be asked to lend a hand. Marion was never short of ideas and always knew what challenges she wanted her characters to face, what their reactions would be and what the ultimate outcome would be. She was not, however, able to cope with the physical demands of sitting typing at a keyboard for hour after hour. My first thought was that I would simply act as a kind of secretary, basically taking dictation from her, but that wasn't her plan at all. She wanted to talk about the "scenes" that unfolded in her head and carried a plotline forward. Dictating would be too slow and tedious for her. She wanted spontaneity to keep things barrelling along at a good pace. So we discussed characters and scenes and I went off to write them up, bringing back a draft printout for Marion to read through. For me, this was the least enjoyable part of the process. I like to think that I always remained calm, acting cool, but it was actually hugely stressful. It was like watching the teacher mark your homework while you're sitting in the dentist's waiting room hearing the whizz of his high-speed drill, and you're having that dream where all your clothes disappear and you're sitting in public stark naked. You've never had that dream? It can't just be me, can it?

Marion read the draft with an editing pen poised in her hand like a guided missile searching for targets to obliterate. It wasn't launched at the paper too often, but Marion also saw straight through my "Mr. Cool" act. She had a way of holding her head to one side and raising an eyebrow as though she was most displeased about something she had just read, then bursting out laughing when she saw me squirming. So much for being cool, but it was good-natured teasing and I was immensely proud that she was happy with what I produced.

I loved chatting with her about her characters and working out what calamities would befall them. As we both became more used to trading thoughts, she was happy to offer me just the start of an idea, leave me to carry it forward a bit and then take it back to add a final flourish which, once she thought it was working, she would do with a big smile, a theatrical wave of the hand and the words: "The End!" It wouldn't be the end of the book, maybe not even the end of a chapter, but it was Marion's way of making sure that little episodes weren't dwelt upon for too long. She liked to keep the story moving forward.

I feel hugely honoured that she trusted me to work with her on Hamish, and in the time we spent together we discussed many more potential plotlines and scenes than were needed for this book. Hamish has far more than his fair share of trouble ahead, but for the meantime he has to contend with the twin demons of jealousy and revenge. The majority of Marion's previous Hamish Macbeth books dealt with human failings of one sort or another. In some, the traits were obvious, in titles like *Death of a Gossip*, *Death of a Bore*, or *Death of a Liar*. Marion was very clear about what she had in mind for this thirty-sixth book, and the title eventually became *Death of a Green-Eyed Monster*.

I hope you enjoy Hamish's latest investigation

as much as I did working with Marion to pull it all together. I will miss all those story sessions, I will always miss Marion, and I count myself as very lucky to have had so much fun with her delving into the world that she created.

R. W. Green, 2022

Death *of a* Green-Eyed Monster

CHAPTER ONE

O, beware, my lord, of jealousy;
It is the green-ey'd monster, which doth mock
The meat it feeds on.
William Shakespeare, *Othello*

She was stunning. Her glossy black hair was drawn back into a high ponytail that dropped in a shining cascade beneath her hat. The shade from the brim did nothing to dim either the sparkle of her blue eyes or the radiance of the perfect smile with which she greeted him.

"Good afternoon, Sergeant," she said, in a soft voice delicately laced with an endearing lilt that might have drifted in from the Western Isles on the summer breeze. "Constable Dorothy McIver reporting for duty."

Hamish Macbeth could scarcely believe his eyes. Was this really his new constable? She stood tall and slim in the sunshine outside his cottage police station in Lochdubh, her outline framed by a blush of purple heather on the hillside behind her. She was wearing a black Police Scotland uniform T-shirt, regulation black cargo trousers. and gleaming black boots. It was the sort of modern police uniform that never looks anything more than bulky, ungainly, and utterly inelegant on most police officers—the kind of uniform Hamish thought made policemen look more like binmen—yet on her it clung to the curves of her shapely, athletic figure as though she were on the catwalk of a high-class Paris fashion house. She even managed to make the ugly service belt at her waist, loaded with handcuffs, a collapsible baton, a torch, and various pouches, look like a designer accessory. He became suddenly aware that he was staring at her and he cast his eyes to the pavement, blushing as vividly as the mountain heather.

"Are you all right, Sergeant?" she asked. "Is there something wrong?"

"No, no. It's chust I neffer...I mean I didn't..." His Highland accent always grew more pronounced when he was flustered. "I didn't expect . . ."

"You didn't expect a woman?" She folded her arms and gave him a reproachful smile.

"No, no . . . no that," he said quickly. "I chust didn't expect . . . yourself until tomorrow. Come away in and we'll have a cup of tea."

She took a step towards the front door of the police station.

"Ah, no that way," Hamish said. "It's jammed with the damp. I've been meaning to see to it. The kitchen door is round the side."

Just as they turned the corner of the building, an odd-looking dog, an assortment of colours and clearly an assortment of breeds, burst through the large flap in the kitchen door and galloped towards them, its big floppy ears flapping like wings and its plume of a tail waving like a flag.

"Lugs!" cried Hamish, stooping to accept the dog's enthusiastic welcome, then swiftly straightening his lanky frame again, laughing as Lugs dashed past him towards Dorothy. "Aye, well, I reckon he finds you a sight more attractive than me!"

"He's adorable!" Dorothy smiled, crouching to

make a fuss of the delighted Lugs. "And who might that be?"

Sonsie, Hamish's pet wild cat, slunk through the flap and eyed Dorothy suspiciously.

"That's Sonsie, my cat."

"She's some size," Dorothy noted. "She looks like a . . ."

"A wild cat?" Hamish interrupted. "Folk often say that, but she's just a big tabby."

Hamish had the Highlanders' relaxed relationship with the truth. Sometimes a sympathetic lie served the world far better than a savage truth, and being a proficient liar made it easier for him to tell when a witness or a suspect was trying to hoodwink him. You can't kid a kidder. He had been knocked a little off balance when he first set eyes on Dorothy, but he was now feeling far steadier in his boots.

"She certainly has the look of a wild cat," said Dorothy, keeping her distance from the beast, as Sonsie's yellow eyes fixed her with a hypnotic gaze. The big cat narrowed her stare to a look of pure malice and then hissed loudly at Dorothy before sauntering off round the back of the cottage, closely followed by Lugs.

"Have you ever actually seen a wild cat? They're as rare as haggis teeth."

"Och, don't, please," she laughed. "That's one to save for the tourists."

She looked even more beautiful when she laughed. Hamish grinned in response. He'd never had much luck with women, or with his constables for that matter, but he was suddenly filled with a thrill of hope that his luck was about to change.

"Well, wild cats are no often spotted," he said quickly, keen to maintain a babble of conversation to disguise the fact that he couldn't keep his eyes off her, "even down at the wild cat sanctuary at Ardnamurchan."

Hamish had once tried to release Sonsie on the Ardnamurchan peninsula but had been so miserable without her that the locals in Lochdubh were glad when he eventually retrieved her. Lugs and Sonsie were his constant companions, and it was an open secret in the village that Sonsie was more than just a large tabby.

"They'll be off down the beach to terrorise the seagulls," said Hamish. "Come ben and we'll get the kettle on."

* * *

Mary Blair stirred a low-calorie sweetener tablet into her tea and stared out of the tall window towards the River Clyde and the Glasgow cityscape. Tea didn't taste the same without real sugar but she was watching her weight, determined to drop a dress size and fit more easily into the new clothes she had been buying. She had been amazed when her husband, Detective Chief Inspector Blair, had encouraged her to visit Glasgow's "Style Mile" around Buchanan Street with a credit card that appeared to have no limit. But Mary hadn't held back. Her drastically improved wardrobe reflected her drastically improved circumstances. When her husband had been slung out of Strathbane and banished to Glasgow, the best she had expected was a damp and decrepit bungalow in some suburban backwater. Yet this apartment in Hyndland was breathtaking.

Mary knew that her husband's salary should always have provided a comfortable lifestyle, but his years of drinking and gambling had often left them struggling with the bills. The wife of a detective chief inspector should not have to worry about having her electricity and phone cut off. She knew that things could turn ugly when she complained, but she knew how to handle men like him. Once, when she told him she needed money to pay the gas bill, he had thrown a few notes at her.

"And if that's not enough"—he had been reeking of cheap whisky and yelling in her face—"you can aye go back on the game!"

She had taken one step back and swung a right hook that laid him out on the living-room floor and blackened his eye. It was true that she had worked the streets. She was no angel, but Hamish Macbeth had saved her from all that and set her up to be married to Blair. That had been her escape from the gutter, but she was still forced to struggle through some hard years. She had seen Blair's gentler side, but more often than not he kept it well hidden, and he loathed Hamish. Yet, often as not, it had been Hamish who had dug Blair out of whatever hole in which his own ineptitude had left him languishing. Hamish had let her husband take the credit for solving countless crimes where Blair had done more to hinder rather than help the investigation and Hamish was the one who had brought the villains to book. Mary owed a great deal to the big Highlander, yet Hamish wanted none of the glory and nothing for himself. His only ambition was to be allowed to get on with his life, the resident police officer in his beloved Lochdubh, looking after his weird dog and cat, his few chickens, and his handful of sheep up on the hillside.

Relaxing into a large armchair, Mary brushed her foot across the carpet where she had been standing, sweeping away the indentations her feet had left in the deep wool pile. New carpets, new furniture, all chosen to suit the large rooms of their new home. The apartment itself was not new but occupied the top floor of a sandstone tenement building that dated back to the end of the nineteenth century, benefiting from the opulence and grandeur through which the Victorian middle classes had declared their wealth. The rooms had high ceilings with elaborate plasterwork in the cornices and ceiling roses, deep skirting boards and elegant fireplaces. The bay in which Mary now sat extended proudly from the corner of the room, topping the bays on the three floors below to form a grand tower crowned with a slated spire. Its four windows looked out over avenues lined with trees—clean streets that had never known the dismal nocturnal trade that had once been Mary's lot.

She settled her cup gently in its saucer on a side table. She was never going back to that life. Her husband appeared to have turned over a new leaf. He was working long hours, not only on duty but also at home, where he had taken one of their three bedrooms as an office. Now she seldom saw him without a glass of whisky in one hand and his phone in the other, renewing old contacts from previous years as a young police officer in Glasgow, talking quietly on long calls that rang back and forth throughout the night. She could never actually trust him, of course—past deceits and the wisdom of experience told her that—but for now there was money in the bank and the future looked rosy. She picked up a glossy brochure and began to browse holiday villas in Malaga.

"I'm afraid I haven't had much of a chance to do any housework since I lost Freddy." Hamish liked to keep things tidy, but the kitchen was not as clean as it might have been. He fanned a copy of last week's *Sunday Post* over one of his kitchen chairs to scatter a little dust and a few crumbs.

"Freddy . . . Constable Ross, that is . . . is now the chef at the Tommel Castle Hotel."

"A chef?" said Dorothy, accepting the seat offered by Hamish. "It must have been nice having someone here to cook for you."

"Aye, we ate well, no doubt about it." Hamish filled the kettle, placing it on the stove. "Are you much of a cook yourself?"

"I can rustle up a few things, but cooking surely isn't part of my duties, is it, Sergeant?"

"No, no, that's not what I meant at all—and by all means call me Hamish when it's just the two of us. We can share all of that kind of domestic stuff. There's not much room around here, though, so you might find it a bit cramped at first."

"That won't be a problem. I will—"

"Sergeant Macbeth!" There was no mistaking the booming voice of Mrs. Wellington, the minister's wife, which thundered through the open kitchen door just before she did so herself. A large woman, clad, as always, in the kind of coarse tweed that looked more like carpet backing than country clothing, Mrs. Wellington glowered at Dorothy. "Who is this?"

"Constable McIver," Hamish explained, "my new assistant."

"I see." Mrs. Wellington exchanged a firm handshake with Dorothy, then turned straight back to Hamish. "We had someone skulking around in the churchyard again last night. After the lead off the church roof, no doubt. I hear they get a fine price for it from the scrap-metal men nowadays."

"Had you called me straight away," said Hamish, "I might have been able to catch them."

"I doubt it. You were nowhere to be found. Perhaps now, however," she said, looking at Dorothy, "female company might tempt you to spend more time here at your police station."

"Oh, I won't be living here," said Dorothy. "Headquarters didn't think that would be appropriate, so they have arranged for me to stay at Mrs. Mackenzie's boardinghouse until I can make other arrangements."

"That's entirely as it should be." Mrs. Wellington took note of Hamish's crestfallen expression. "Now, what about these thieves, Macbeth?"

"How much did they strip from the roof?"

"Nothing. I chased them off into the dark and heard them drive away in a van."

"It'll be those scunners up from Strathbane again. I'll have a word with the local police.

They'll make sure the lead burglars know we're watching for them."

"Please do. Good day, Miss McIver."

Mrs. Wellington departed in a rustle of tweed, and Hamish turned to Dorothy.

"So you're staying at the Mackenzie place?"

"Yes, temporarily. Is it all right there?"

"Aye, it's fine. She doesn't have what you might call 'top-class clientele'—mainly forestry workers and the like—but it should do you until we can sort something else out for you."

"Right. Well, I'll get back there now and finish getting my things out of my car, if that's okay?"

"Aye, yes, of course, and . . . well, would you be needing any help with that?"

"No, I can manage, thanks."

As she left, she flashed him another smile, and, had Hamish been a hopeless romantic, his heart would have melted. But part of him was, and part of it did.

By the time Mrs. Wellington had marched back to the manse, she had passed the time of day with Mrs. Maclean, the wife of Archie, a local fisherman; Mrs. Brodie, wife of the village doctor; and Mrs. Patel, who ran the village store with her husband. That was more than enough to ensure that by the time she had boiled the kettle and sat down with a cup of tea and a copy of *Life and Work*, the Church of Scotland magazine, everyone in the entire area surrounding Lochdubh knew that Hamish Macbeth's new constable was but a slip of a girl who looked more like she should be playing a police officer in a TV soap than actually catching real criminals. And how was he supposed to maintain law and order throughout Sutherland with such a distraction filling his every thought day and night? He was only human, after all, only a man, and she such a temptress. So it was that Dorothy McIver became branded a "scarlet woman" before most people in Lochdubh had ever even clapped eyes on her.

The following morning, Dorothy reported to the police station bright and early to find Hamish standing by the open front door, sipping coffee from a mug, Lugs and Sonsie at his feet. Hamish had spotted her long before she reached the station. She looked every bit as lovely as he remembered, and he had spent most of the night thinking of her—her blue eyes, her smile, her every graceful movement—until he reached the point when he was beginning to believe that he had imagined her.

"Good morning," she said. "I see you've managed to unstick the front door." Lugs bounded up to her and she stooped to ruffle his ears. Sonsie simply glowered at her.

"Aye, it just needed a wee bit of encouragement." Hamish had spent hours trimming the bottom of the door, rehanging it and giving it a fresh coat of blue paint. He ran his free hand through his fiery red hair, noticed the dried paint stains on his fingers, and shoved the hand in his pocket. "Will you be wanting some breakfast?"

"I've already eaten, thanks, but a coffee would be nice."

"Come away in, then," said Hamish. He turned and stepped into the small hallway, closing the door to the office. He hadn't yet had time to spruce that up, but the kitchen was now an immaculately clean, cosy haven. He was fairly sure Dorothy approved, although neither mentioned the transformation. Over coffee he explained a little about Lochdubh and the vast area of Sutherland that was their "patch," then they took a walk through the village, along the seawall. The sun, despite having lost the heat of high summer, broke through the high white clouds, warming the mountainsides around the loch. The tide was out, exposing the widest expanse of beach, patrolled by a scattering of white gulls. Lugs and Sonsie dashed among them and the gulls took to the air, screeching in protest.

To the side of the Patels' shop, they came across Mrs. Patel, pacing back and forth beside a small van, wringing her hands with worry.

"Is there a problem, Mrs. Patel?" Hamish asked.

"Can you help, Hamish? I've been such a dunderheid—locked myself out of the van," she said in a hushed voice. "The engine's running and the keys are inside. All that petrol being wasted. I dare not tell my husband I've been so stupid. He's working in the shop."

"Have you not a spare set?"

"Aye, of course. They're in my handbag—on the passenger seat."

"I have a tool in my Land Rover that we can maybe force down through the top of the door and pop the lock."

"Will it cause any damage?"

"No more than a wee scratch at most."

"But he'll go daft if we scratch his precious van!"

"I'm sure he wouldn't. He's not some kind of monster," said Hamish, looking over the van, which, to him, seemed as scraped and scuffed as a comfortable pair of old shoes. "Are you that sure he'd even notice?"

"Don't worry, Mrs. Patel," said Dorothy. "This should do the trick." She pulled a length of nylon cord from her pocket. In the middle of the cord was a small loop. Gently easing the string in between the rubber door seals, she used a sawing motion to drag one end along the top of the door and the other down the side, carefully lowering the loop towards the pop-up button lock on the top of the door trim. Once she had worked the loop around the button, she pulled outwards on both ends of the string to tighten the loop, then upwards to lift the button and open the lock.

"Thank you, thank you, thank you, Constable," said Mrs. Patel, climbing into the van.

"No problem," said Dorothy, "and you're fine calling me Dorothy, Mrs. Patel."

Showering Dorothy with thanks and praise, Mrs. Patel set off for the cash and carry in Strathbane.

"A neat trick," said Hamish.

"We got lucky." Dorothy smiled. "It doesn't always work."

Walking on through the village, Hamish spotted the alarming, familiar forms of Nessie and Jessie Currie approaching. He glanced left and right but there was nowhere to run and nowhere to hide.

"Crivens," he muttered to Dorothy. "It's the Currie twins. Brace yourself, Dorothy."

"Sergeant Macbeth!" shrieked Nessie at a volume that belied her diminutive stature. Her sister, Jessie, was the same size, had precisely the same tightly permed grey hair, exactly the same thick glasses, and an identical camel-hair coat. "We want to report a crime!"

"A crime!" repeated her sister.

"What crime?" Hamish asked.

"Last night in our garden there was a peeping Tom!"

"Peeping Tom!" chorused Jessie.

"We'd have none of this sort of thing in Lochdubh if you weren't such a lazy layabout!" Nessie ranted. "Keeking in through our curtains he was, and flashing."

"Flashing!" Jessie agreed.

"What do you mean, 'flashing'?" asked Hamish.

"Flashing a torch," said Nessie. "Very bright it was."

"Most peeping Toms don't advertise their presence with flashing lights. What do you think, Constable McIver?" Hamish introduced Dorothy.

"Would you like me to come and sit with you in the evening, ladies?" asked Dorothy. "Maybe then we could catch your intruder."

"A police officer in our house?" said Nessie, aghast. "What would people think? We would be the talk of the village."

"Talk of the village!"

"Maybe I could come in ordinary clothes," said Dorothy gently, "not in uniform. That wouldn't attract attention—and if I came after dark, no one would see me at all."

The sisters looked at each other and nodded.

"That would be acceptable. We will expect you this evening. We are very glad that, unlike your sergeant, you seem to be a proper police officer and not, like people have been saying, just some fluffy flibbertigibbet."

"Flibbertigibbet!"

And with a curt "good morning," the Currie twins departed, their matching brown leather shoes marching precisely in time.

"You're sure you want to do that?" asked Hamish once the camel-hair figures were at a safe distance. "I'd rate that as above and beyond the call of duty."

"I feel like I need to go the extra mile if I'm ever going to be accepted here." Dorothy smiled at him. "I need to win hearts and minds."

Hamish turned and called to Lugs and Sonsie. Win hearts and minds? By now he was pretty sure she had won his heart already, and he didn't mind a bit. They walked back to the station, where Hamish loaded Lugs and Sonsie into the Land Rover.

"Let's see a bit of the wider patch," he said, heading for the humpbacked bridge that led out of Lochdubh.

The roads were quiet, the flood of summer tourists having dwindled to a trickle, and Hamish pointed out various landmarks while he drove. They pulled into a small car park by the side of Loch Assynt, and Dorothy walked a few paces towards the water, shielding her eyes from the glare of the sun reflecting off the surface. To the west she could see the distant peaks and rock faces of the Quinag mountains basking in the sunshine, and to the east the towering presence of Ben More Assynt. Hamish let his pets out to run around.

"It's lovely here," she said. "It feels so . . . old."

"There's no doubt about that," Hamish agreed. "Around here we have some of the oldest rocks in the world. The tops of these mountains stood out above the ice sheet when everything else was buried under glaciers.

"Down that way at the head of the loch is Inchnadamph, and beyond it the Bone Caves where they found human remains over five thousand years old and animal bones they say are up to ten times as old, including polar bears."

"Polar bears?" Dorothy looked sceptical. "Would you be pulling my leg, Sergeant Macbeth?"

"Not at all," Hamish laughed. "Every word is true. And down there"—he pointed to a promontory where stood a ruined stone tower and ancient castle walls slowly crumbling into the loch—"is Ardvreck Castle, once home to the Macleods of Assynt."

"What happened to it?"

"It was struck by lightning over two hundred and fifty years ago. There are those who believe it was an act of God to cleanse the area of the Devil's influence."

"The Devil? In a place as beautiful as this?"

"Aye, Auld Clootie himself. Follow the loch west and beyond, out over the Minch to the islands, and you will come to the Macleods' ancestral home in the Hebrides. Assynt was their foothold on the mainland, with Mackay country to the north and the Mackenzies to the south.

"The first Laird wanted the castle built quickly to defend Assynt against the Mackays and Mackenzies, but labour was scarce and the stonemasons struggled in terrible weather. The Devil came to hear of his troubles and appeared to the Laird in the part-built castle, offering to complete Ardvreck in return for his soul. The Laird was not prepared to spend eternity in the fiery pits of Hell and tried to negotiate with the Devil. Just then the Laird's daughter, Eimhir, strolled by the window. She was a rare beauty and fair took the Devil's breath away. He instantly offered to finish the castle in return for her hand in marriage. The Laird agreed, the castle was finished, and Eimhir, as was the custom in those days, was told to prepare for her wedding, without knowing whom she was to marry.

"A grand wedding was planned in the castle's great hall, but on the morning of her wedding day, Eimhir discovered who was about to take her as his wife. She was horrified and hurled herself from the high tower into the depths of the loch. Yet Eimhir did not drown. She hid from the Devil in caverns in the deepest part of the loch, becoming the seldom-seen Mermaid of Assynt.

"Whenever the waters of the loch rise, turning yon spit of land into an island, it is said to be because Eimhir is weeping a flood of tears for her lost life on dry land."

"That's quite a tale." Dorothy smiled. "Is that the sort of story you were brought up on?"

"Not really," Hamish admitted. "It's mainly from Wikipedia. The tourists love all that stuff."

Dorothy laughed, then pointed to another ruin on the shore of the loch. "And what's that? Looks like it must have been a big mansion."

"That it was," said Hamish. "The Mackenzies eventually seized Ardvreck but the new Laird's wife found the castle too draughty, so he built her a fine house. They entertained with great feasts and dancing until one Saturday night when midnight was approaching, one of the pipers refused to continue playing because he would not desecrate the Sabbath. He was cast out into the snow and the revellers carried on drinking and dancing. That night the house was burned to the ground and the lone piper was the only one present that evening who survived. Some say that, when the snow lies thick on the ground on dark winter nights, you can sometimes see lights in the house and hear the skirl of the pipes and the dancers laughing and whooping."

"Does everything on our patch have a story to tell?"

"Pretty much." Hamish grinned. "And how about you? They sent me your police service record, but there's nothing much in it about your background."

Dorothy lowered her eyes to the ground and Hamish felt a sudden chill, as though a cloud had passed in front of the sun.

"There's not that much to tell," she said quietly. "A succession of foster homes, never knew any real family, and then I joined the police and started to make something of myself. What's that? Sounds like a . . ."

Hamish turned towards the road in time to see a low, sleek, red sports car come screaming past, disappearing in the blink of an eye round a bend that took the road north towards Unapool.

"Bloody hell!" Hamish breathed. "Quick—let's get after him." He called his pets back to the car.

"You surely don't expect to catch that car," said Dorothy, climbing into the Land Rover and fastening her seat belt, "in this old heap?"

"This old heap," said Hamish, frowning at her, "will do just fine, for I well know where he's headed."

The tyres spat out a shower of gravel as Hamish gunned the Land Rover's engine, swinging out of the car park onto the road. He snatched up his phone and pressed a speed-dial number.

"Dougie, incoming. Hold on to him as long as you can. I'm on my way."

"Who's Dougie?"

"Dougie Tennant is a mechanic. He has a petrol station on the road to Scourie. That car will want to stop there. There's a right big old-fashioned clock on the front of the building and the driver will want to take a photograph with the clock in the background to prove how fast he got there. My guess is he's doing the North Coast Five Hundred."

"The tourist route?"

"Aye, it's intended for tourists, and they can take a week or more to travel the whole route, but there's some as like to challenge their pals to see how fast they can cover the five hundred miles. Our man in the red car will have come from Inverness, or Lochcarron, or wherever else along the route his racing pals have made their base."

"Most of these roads aren't great for fast driving."

"No, they're not, but these idiots don't realise that until it's too late. Dougie will switch off his petrol pumps and pretend there's a fault until we get there."

Half an hour later, Hamish pulled up into the forecourt of a small filling station and picked up the radio handset.

"Need to check out that car with head-quarters," he said.

"You don't have a computer in the car to do that?" Dorothy commented, looking round the cab of the Land Rover.

"We don't always get good enough Wi-Fi up here for it to work properly," he said, and then clicked the radio handset. "Macbeth here, Alex. Can you run a check for me on a red, um..."

Dorothy held out a hand, motioning Hamish to pass her the radio.

"Red Ferrari GTC4Lusso," she reported, "registration number . . ."

Hamish stepped out of the Land Rover and approached the red Ferrari, whose driver was having a heated debate with Dougie.

"What appears to be the problem, sir?" he asked.

The driver turned towards him. He looked to be in his mid-thirties, a small, thin man with the eyes of a weasel and lank, dark hair.

"This oik won't sell me any fuel," wailed the man in a voice that had the plaintive top-drawer trill Hamish had only ever heard from the mouths of painfully affluent English tourists born and bred so far south of Lochdubh that they might as well have come from another planet.

"It's not my fault," grumbled Dougie, shrugging his skinny shoulders and wiping his hands on an oily rag. "The electric's gone off."

"Away and see if you can fix it, Dougie," said Hamish. Then he turned to the driver. "We saw you down by Loch Assynt. You might not use up so much of your petrol if you didn't drive so fast. This car can't get much more than . . ."

"Fifteen miles to the gallon the way you were driving." Dorothy joined them by the Ferrari, running a hand gently along its gleaming flank. "This is the vee-twelve, right? Four-wheel drive, four-wheel steering. Good for two hundred miles an hour."

"Two hundred and eight," the driver corrected, with a greasy smile.

"But not on my patch." Hamish rounded on the man. "Name?"

"Anthony Masterson de Witte."

"Constable?" Hamish glanced towards Dorothy, who was lavishing the car with a look bordering on adoration. He suddenly felt decidedly irritated. She clearly loved the car, but it didn't deserve that sort of attention. It was only metal and glass, after all. She shouldn't be admiring a car that way, he thought. That's the sort of look that should be reserved for . . . me? Surely I can't be jealous, he scolded himself. Surely not jealous of a car?

"The car checks out, Sergeant," said Dorothy. "This gentleman is the registered keeper."

Hamish turned to the man and lambasted

him over his reckless driving, berating him about putting other people's lives in danger just for fun, castigating him for endangering livestock and wildlife, and delivering a lengthy, high-volume lecture about slow-moving camper vans and tractors that can be lurking round any bend. His lecture lasted almost twenty minutes, by which time, he knew, any bet the driver had made with his chums was well and truly lost. At some point during his tirade, Dougie restored the power to the pumps.

"Now fill it up," Hamish growled, "but if I hear about you driving like an eejit anywhere on my patch ever again, I will hunt you down and impound your shiny Ferrari. They have to park all sorts of things in the yard at Strathbane—trucks, tractors, snow ploughs—and they're none too careful about it. By the time you get your silly wee car back it will look like the Scots Guards have marched over it in tackety boots!"

He hauled himself back into the Land Rover, followed by Dorothy, who took one last, lingering look at the Ferrari.

"Impressive," was all she said.

"Yon stupid car?"

"No, you. I thought at one point he was going to wet himself."

"If I'd given him the full works, he'd have done worse than that."

"You seem to care a lot about everything up here in the back of beyond."

"I do. This is God's own country. Those that are born here choose to stay because they love the place. Those who move here and don't ruin themselves with the drink or aren't frightened off by the winter weather, also stay because they love the place. Looking after them, and looking after our patch of Sutherland, is a thing I care about a great deal."

"You really do, don't you, Hamish?"

"Aye. Now, how is it," he asked, "that you know so much about cars?"

"Not really a woman's territory, you mean? I spent a bit of time out on the road with the traffic patrols around Glasgow"—she looked sideways at him—"and I like nice things. Nice cars, nice clothes. Is there anything wrong with that?"

"Not at all." Hamish shrugged. "We'd best head back. You have an appointment with the Currie twins—hearts and minds to win."

Dorothy caught sight of Sonsie in the rear-view mirror, yellow eyes radiating hostility. She shot the cat a look as cold as ice, noting with satisfaction its momentary flinch. Sonsie's heart and mind might never be won, but the wild cat needed to know there was a new big cat on the block.

CHAPTER TWO

She was a Phantom of delight
When first she gleamed upon my sight;
A lovely Apparition, sent
To be a moment's ornament . . .
William Wordsworth, "Perfect
Woman"

"She's done what? Why did you let her do that? I ken that better than anybody, but we must stick to the plan!" Blair sounded angry. Mary knew how the tone of his voice wavered when he was trying to hold his temper in check, and it was wavering now. She stood in the hall, hesitating by the bedroom her husband used as his office, frozen in the shaft of electric light cast across the carpet from the part-opened door. She was waiting until it sounded safe to enter. Even though the door stood just a few inches ajar, she could hear him as plainly as if he were yelling in her ear rather than down the telephone.

"The teuchters never miss a thing! They see everybody that comes and goes. They're aye watching—nothing better to do. She has to take it nice and calm!" Blair's voice was suddenly louder and the door was yanked wide open. He stood in the doorway scowling at Mary. "I'll call you back." He hung up. "What are you doing lurking here—listening at keyholes, are you?"

"No, I . . . I didn't really need to listen at the keyhole. The door was open."

"You know what I mean—eavesdropping! Spying on me!"

"Why would I want to do that? I've no interest in your police work. It's getting late and I just wanted to know if you needed a top-up before I went off to bed." She offered him the bottle of Glenlivet she was holding. He snatched it out of her hand and slammed the door in her face.

If that was police work, Mary thought to herself, then I'm bloody Kojak. He was definitely up to something.

* * *

Hamish was in shirtsleeves, enjoying the early morning sunshine while cleaning the front windows of the police station. He had worked himself into a sweat, keen to get the job done before Dorothy arrived. He smiled and shook his head, scolding himself. Not everything should be about Dorothy, he told himself, yet he knew that he thought of nothing now without including her. Every picture that popped into his head had Dorothy in it somewhere. When he thought about feeding his chickens, she was there with a bowl of grain under her arm. When he thought about driving up beyond Kinlochbervie and visiting the beaches at Oldshoremore or even Sandwood Bay, she was there in the Land Rover beside him and there walking on the sand with Lugs and Sonsie. Thinking about her showing up for work this morning was giving him butterflies in his stomach. Hamish Macbeth, he told himself sternly, grow up. Stop acting like a lovesick loon!

"Hard at it, eh, Hamish?" came the unmistakeable growl of Archie Maclean. "You've missed a wee bit there at the top. Making it all bonnie for the new lassie, are you?"

"No, no, not at all," Hamish blustered, rinsing his cloth in the bucket. "Just about time this was done. And she's not a lassie—she is an experienced police officer. Should you not have your boat out this morning? The weather won't get any better."

"I was up and out before dawn, while you were still snorin' your heid off."

"A good catch this morning?" Dorothy came walking down the street towards them. "It's Archie, isn't it? I heard your boat coming in earlier."

"Aye, a fair catch, miss. Some sea bass and a good haul o' mackerel."

"Mackerel? Late in the year for mackerel, I'd have thought," Dorothy commented. "Have they not headed south?"

"This will be the last of them, I reckon," said Archie, pulling a brown paper package from inside his loose-fitting denim jacket and offering it to Dorothy. "I've a pair here for you both."

"Thank you, Archie. I love mackerel."

Archie bade them farewell and wandered off towards the harbour, the legs of his wide jeans flapping in the breeze.

"Archie's going a bit mad with the baggy clothes," Hamish said as they watched him go.

"He was forever dressed in jackets and trousers that were too tight because his wife boiled all the laundry in a big old copper and shrank it. Then he came into some money, bought her a washing machine, and he's never known such comfort."

"He's certainly a character," said Dorothy.

"And how is it that you know so much about fish now as well as cars?"

"Hearts and minds, Hamish, remember?" Dorothy laughed. "You're not the only one who can use Wikipedia! I'll pop these fish in the fridge and get the kettle on. I need to fill you in on the Currie sisters' snooper."

Hamish emptied his bucket onto the base of a hydrangea in the small front garden, wrung out his cloth, and marvelled yet again at the beauty that was PC Dorothy McIver.

"I had a look in their garden and it was clear that someone had been standing in one of their flowerbeds near the corner of the house," Dorothy explained, sitting in the kitchen with Hamish, each sipping coffee from a steaming mug. "I think it was linked to the lead thieves Mrs. Wellington scared off at the kirk. Maybe a lookout."

"You may be right," said Hamish, picturing

where the Curries' cottage sat. "From that corner of the Curries' garden you have a clear view of the kirk and you can see up and down the road as far as the bridge. It's a good lookout point and a good signalling point—the flashing torch."

"Exactly. You need a van if you're going to carry lead away, but you can't drive anything over the bridge into Lochdubh without being seen from the manse or the windows in one of the village houses. So the signal was to say that the coast was clear—house lights out or curtains drawn. Then the van could come in quietly, with its lights off, maybe even rolling down the street with the engine off."

"Could be. I spoke to Jimmy Anderson at Strathbane and he thinks it might be strangers to the area. If that's so, they might well try again."

"We'll be ready for them."

"How? There's only two of us. We can't stay on watch all night every night and still get on with the rest of our work."

"I've enlisted the Currie twins." Dorothy smiled. "Persuaded them that we clever women could outsmart the nasty men that were coming to steal from our kirk. They'll be looking out for the lookout."

"We'd better talk to Mrs. Wellington . . ."

"Already done it," Dorothy interrupted. "She'll be in an armchair by the window overlooking the churchyard."

"Good work," said Hamish. "Between the lot of us, we'll spot them if they try sneaking into Lochdubh again."

His mobile phone rang, and Dorothy made a fuss of Lugs while he answered it. Sonsie was perched on the window ledge outside the kitchen, staring in at Dorothy.

"Silas," said Hamish. "Aye, she's here with me now. We'll come over to the hotel. It will give me a chance to show Dor . . . Constable McIver where it is. See you in a few minutes."

They loaded Lugs and Sonsie into the Land Rover and set off for the Tommel Castle Hotel.

"So two of your former constables now work at the hotel?" said Dorothy.

"Aye, Silas is their security man and Freddy is their chef. Before that Clarry was the chef—he also used to be one of my PCs. I've lost a few to the hotel and catering trade. Dick Fraser married a Polish girl, Anka, and they set up their own bakery over in Braikie. Willie Lamont married the daughter of the local Italian restaurant owner and he works there now."

"Is the Italian any good?"

"The best. Tell you what, you've not had much of a welcome to Lochdubh, so I'll treat you to a meal there tonight."

Hamish turned into Tommel Castle's stone gateway and they emerged from an avenue of tall, bushy rhododendrons into the hotel car park. He pulled up near the imposing front door and let Lugs and Sonsie out. They immediately dashed off down the side of the building towards the kitchen where they knew that Freddy would have some scraps waiting for them. Hamish saw Dorothy looking up at the grandeur of Tommel Castle's battlements, turrets, and spires. It was an impressive building, yet this was no ancient fortification. The battlements were a Victorian conceit, the castle having been built as a country residence at a time when Queen Victoria, and the expanding railway network, had made owning a Highland retreat the height of fashion. Hamish had always considered Tommel to be a minia-ture version of Dunrobin Castle near Golspie, the seat of the Sutherland clan. Tommel had nowhere near the 189 rooms of Dunrobin, but it was designed in the same unashamedly romantic style—part solid stone fortress and part French fantasy chateau.

"This is a lovely place," said Dorothy quietly.

"It is that," Hamish agreed. "Used to be a private house, but the owner turned it into a hotel when the running costs started to get out of hand."

They walked into the reception area, where Silas Dunbar was waiting for them. Compared to Hamish, Silas seemed far too small ever to have been a police officer, but he had scraped through the selection process at minimum regulation height. The policeman's life, however, had not been for him and he had been very glad when Colonel George Halburton-Smythe, owner of Tommel Castle, had offered him a job as the hotel's security man.

Hamish introduced Dorothy and was pleased to see that Silas greeted her with a confident smile. He had changed since his time on the force, when the despicable Blair had made life unbearable for him. Silas now appeared far more self-assured. His shoulders sat square, not cringing forward, and he even seemed just a wee bit taller. Silas ordered coffee in the hotel bar and the barman brought it over just as Freddy Ross, wearing his chef's whites, arrived to join them.

Tall and lanky, with thick dark hair and a lean face, Freddy was a far better chef than he had ever been a policeman. He placed a tray of fresh croissants on the table in front of them, along with side plates, butter, and home-made jam.

"These are delicious," said Dorothy, biting into a buttered croissant and sweeping a fallen flake of pastry off her trouser leg.

"Simple enough when you've a kitchen as good as the one here." Freddy grinned. "You've a touch of the islands in your voice. I'm from Barra originally."

"I've not been to the Hebrides for a long time," said Dorothy.

"So what is it that you want to talk to us about?" Hamish wiped croissant crumbs from his mouth with the back of his hand. Dorothy handed him a napkin.

"Freddy and I were having a quick drink at the bar there last night," said Silas, "when a woman came into reception. Mr. Johnson, the manager, was behind the desk."

"It was late," Freddy added. "I had closed the

kitchen and Silas was about to do his last rounds and lock up. The woman started talking like she wanted to check in."

"That might be unusual at that time of night," said Hamish, "but it's not a crime."

"Of course not," said Silas, "but then she started asking about you, Dorothy."

"Wanted to know if anyone had seen you, if you were staying here," Freddy said, "or if you were staying somewhere else in town."

"What did she look like?" Hamish asked.

"Small, blonde hair, probably middle-aged but looked younger, well dressed," said Freddy.

Hamish turned to Dorothy and raised an eyebrow. She shook her head, looking mystified. "Doesn't sound like anyone I know," she said.

"Did you speak to her?" Hamish asked.

"No, but we could hear her fine," Silas explained. "Glasgow accent. When she spotted us listening, she just said 'Forget it' and left. By the time we walked over to the front door, she was in her car and away."

"What kind of car?" Dorothy asked.

"Couldn't really see," said Freddy. "Disappeared into the dark on the drive before we got a good look. Might have been blue."

"I'm pretty sure there was someone else in the car with her—a driver—who was sitting waiting for her outside," added Silas. "That's how she managed to get away so quickly."

"I think we'd better be having a word with Mr. Johnson," said Hamish.

"Really?" Dorothy objected. "It doesn't sound like something to waste time on."

"While we're here," Hamish insisted, "it won't take long. Is he in his office?"

Hamish led Dorothy into the entrance hall, where the receptionist nodded politely from behind her desk. The office door was at the end of the hall, past the ornate oak staircase. Hamish knocked and entered, then froze. Priscilla Halburton-Smythe, daughter of the hotel's owner, sat opposite the manager, a litter of bills, invoices, and receipts covering most of the desk between them. Priscilla's father sat to the side of the desk.

"I need a quick word, Mr. Johnson," said Hamish, "about the woman who came to the hotel late last night."

"Oh, hello, Priscilla," said Priscilla, teasing Hamish. "So nice to see you again. Are you up from London for long?"

"Aye, right, hello, Priscilla," Hamish said, running his hand through his hair.

"Aren't you going to introduce us to your colleague?"

"Of course, aye, of course." Hamish was feeling decidedly uncomfortable. Priscilla looked stunning, as always. Her smooth blonde hair and slim figure had always attracted admiring glances from men and women whenever she and Hamish had been out together. Her sharp wit completed an irresistible package that had led to them becoming engaged, although Hamish had ultimately broken it off. "This is Constable McIver, my new assistant."

Priscilla stood, joining the two men who were already on their feet, and they shook hands with Dorothy.

"He may sometimes forget his manners," Priscilla said to Dorothy, smiling, "but he's really very civilised in most other respects. How are you finding Lochdubh?"

"Still getting my bearings," said Dorothy. "Not quite settled in yet."

"It might take a bit of work to get all the locals on your side," Priscilla advised, "but I'm sure you can charm them."

"So about this woman last night . . ." Hamish launched into a series of questions that Mr. Johnson answered with an account identical to that of Freddy and Silas. The colonel studied Dorothy. In his opinion, she was an exceptionally good-looking young filly. Perhaps she lacked some of the refined sophistication of his daughter—she might be a little too tall to be as elegant as Priscilla—but he was sure Macbeth would find her attractive. Or would he? The colonel had never understood why the big Highlander had called off the engagement. It had been an excruciating affront to his family that his manifest snobbery had made agonisingly difficult to endure. Yet he still couldn't help liking Hamish Macbeth.

"Is this mystery woman up to no good?" asked the colonel.

"It's most likely nothing." Dorothy smiled. "Storm in a teacup."

In the Land Rover on the way back into Lochdubh, Hamish questioned Dorothy again about why someone would have been asking about her.

"It's no big deal," said Dorothy. "Probably somebody living up here that I haven't seen for years. There will be a simple explanation. Priscilla seemed very nice."

"She is," Hamish agreed. "At one time we were engaged to be married, but I called it all off."

"Mmm—that must be tricky to deal with."

"No really. She spends a lot of time down south. Comes up for holidays and to go through the accounts with her dad and Mr. Johnson. We're still good friends."

"So she's involved in the hotel business?"

"She's some kind of computer programmer, but she knows all about Tommel Castle. She'll inherit the hotel one day."

"What? The whole lot? No brothers or sisters?"

"No, I suppose everything will go to Priscilla."

"Lucky, lucky girl." Dorothy's jaw tightened and her whole face took on a hard look of rising bitterness. "Why on earth did you drop her, Hamish?"

"It just wouldn't have worked out between us." The phrase came easily to Hamish. He had, after all, used it a hundred times before. What he couldn't say was that, despite her beauty and intelligence making her seem like every man's desire, desire was precisely what Priscilla lacked. She had brought no passion to their relationship, and her cold, unresponsive lovemaking had convinced Hamish that she was not the woman to whom he could devote himself. Yet, from time to time, he still dreamt of what might have been with a more spirited, amorous Priscilla. The thought flashed through his mind at that very moment, only the woman in his arms this time was not Priscilla—it was Dorothy.

"What are you thinking?" Dorothy's face was transformed by her radiant smile.

"Och, no ... nothing ... I was chust ..." The sibilance creeping into his accent showed that, once again, she had caught him off guard. The radio crackled and Hamish snatched up the handset.

"What is it, Alex?"

"Some bairn stuck up a tree in Lochdubh and nobody can find you."

"We're just on our way back from Tommel Castle. There in one minute." Hamish slotted the handset back in its holder. "That'll be the McWilliams boy again. Loves climbing the tree, then gets scared and can't get down. Aye, look, there he is."

A small crowd had gathered beneath an ancient sycamore tree, all craning their necks to see a small boy sitting on a branch far out from the trunk and almost thirty feet from the ground. He was no more than four years old, dressed in shorts and a play-stained blue T-shirt. Hamish strode over to where the boy's mother stood, fists clenched in anger, alternately looking up to yell at her son, then down at the ground to avoid the stares of others and the shame of him having caused such a scene.

"Don't worry, Margaret, we'll get him down," Hamish assured her.

"I've told him not to climb the tree," she muttered.

"I know, Margaret, but boys will be boys, eh?" Hamish looked up and called to the boy. "Malcolm! That's a grand height you've reached this time. Don't be feared, now. Come away down, nice and slow, and I've some sweeties here for you."

"I've told him not to take sweeties from strangers," said Margaret.

"It's a handsome tree," said Dorothy, following the branches with her gaze, up to where Malcolm sat gently sobbing, tears rolling down his cheeks.

"The Faraway Tree," said Hamish. "The seeds spin like helicopters when they fall. The bairns throw a seed into the wind and before it reaches the ground they make a wish to travel somewhere far away. It's been here as long as anyone can remember. Some say it's over four hundred years old. The bairns challenge each other to climb it," he added, sighing. "I'd better go up after him."

"Those branches might not take your weight," said Dorothy, taking off her hat and unfastening her service belt. "I'll do it."

"She's a game girl." Angela Brodie, the local doctor's wife, stood close to Hamish, watching Dorothy swing herself up onto a branch stout enough to bear her weight and then make her way higher, with agile grace, towards the trembling Malcolm.

"She is that," Hamish agreed.

"Pretty, too," added Angela. "I think this one's a keeper, Hamish."

With Hamish left wondering whether she meant he should keep her as a constable or as something more, the small crowd fell into a hush. Dorothy was shuffling sideways along the branch towards Malcolm. She sat next to him, spoke very gently, then pulled a smartphone out of her pocket, tapping the screen and showing it to the frightened boy. She spoke again, he nodded, and she swung one leg over the branch to sit astride it with her back to Malcolm. She reached back with one arm to steady him and he flung his arms around her neck, wrapping his legs around her waist. Then she carried him slowly and carefully to the ground, where the onlookers burst into a round of applause. Margaret McWilliams thanked Dorothy profusely and then marched her son off down the street, uttering dire threats about what would happen to him if he ever shamed her like that in public again.

"Good job," said Hamish. "What was that magic trick you did with the phone?"

"Pulled up a picture of a koala bear with its baby." Dorothy laughed. "That's how they carry their young, so he knew what to do."

News of the incident at the Faraway Tree spread quickly, as news tends to do in the Highlands, and wherever Hamish went with Dorothy, children would point, cheer, and chant, "Koala Cop! Koala Cop!" Hamish had never known anything like it. In the past, when people had called for police help, they were usually pleased to see him;

now whenever he went out on a call on his own, the first thing anyone said to him was, "Where's Dorothy?," disappointed if he hadn't brought his glamorous constable.

Just over a week later, they received a furtive late-night call from the Currie twins and made it to the church in time to collar three of the lead gang. Two more were arrested in their van on the road near Strathbane after Hamish phoned to alert local officers. Dorothy's campaign to win "hearts and minds" could not have gone better, and they decided to celebrate with an off-duty night out at the Italian restaurant.

"Willie!" Hamish called as they entered. His former PC looked up from where he was polishing the brass rail that ran along the bar. "A bottle of Valpolicella!"

"No, Willie," Dorothy said. "I saw a lovely bottle of Amarone on the wine list last time we were here. Do you still have some?"

"I do indeed." Willie grinned. Not many people opted for his most expensive wine.

"And can we sit here by the window? It's a bit nicer than Hamish's usual table."

"Of course you can." Willie made a show of flipping his duster over a chair for Dorothy and offered to take her coat before she sat. "My, this is a fine leather jacket. Never felt such soft leather."

"Thank you," said Dorothy. "It's Italian. I thought it would be appropriate." She was wearing a low-cut white silk blouse, gently faded jeans, and shining black leather boots. Her hair fell to her shoulders in dark waves, and Hamish could not believe any woman had ever looked more beautiful.

Willie lit a candle on the table. The flame guttered momentarily. Outside it was growing dark and a breeze was beginning to blow in off the loch. The many panes in the restaurant's front window no longer fitted their frames quite as snugly as they once had, allowing a draught to slip through.

"Reckon we've seen the end of that late summer," said Hamish.

"It was beautiful while it lasted, but I hear that winter days up here can be wonderful, too."

"The weather can be right harsh, but there are days when it is so cold, clear, and still that it fair takes your breath away. So tell me, Dorothy, what made you decide to come here? It wasn't just a posting. Jimmy Anderson told me you volunteered."

"I did. I wanted to see what it was like living here."

"It's a far cry from where you were in Glasgow. We don't have the shops, the nightlife, the restaurants, the theatres, the . . ."

"And that's really why I wanted to come here," said Dorothy. She sipped the taste of wine that Willie poured for her, smiled, and nodded for him to carry on pouring. "I wanted away from the seedy side of police work in the city—the violence, the gangs, the corruption. I like having nice things. What I want most now is a nice life. I think I can find that here, but not at Mrs. Mackenzie's!"

She laughed. They clinked glasses and enjoyed their wine.

"Surely she's not been giving you a hard time?" Hamish asked.

"No, nothing like that. It's just really basic there—pretty grotty, in fact. She only allows one bath a week. Forestry workers or ditch diggers might be able to put up with that, but I'm paying her extra so that I can wash properly. She offered to do some laundry for me but she dries the washing on a pulley in the kitchen, so my clothes come back smelling of chips and fried bacon. I need to move out of there."

"There is room for you at the station house." He prayed he didn't sound as hopeful as he felt.

"Can you imagine the gossip if I moved in there with you, however innocent and above board it might be? No, I was thinking that, since two of your former PCs already work there, we could negotiate a good rate for me at the Tommel Castle."

"That's not a bad idea. They're coming into their quiet time anyway, so they might be glad to have you."

Within days Dorothy had moved into a bright and spacious room at the hotel and over the next few weeks she and Hamish became almost inseparable. He guided her around the farthest-flung outposts of their patch, from the towering cliffs of Cape Wrath in the north to the gentle shoreline at the southern reaches of Loch Shin, and he showed her all the local sights, from the Old Man of Stoer rock stack standing fast against the Atlantic in the west to the dolphins playing in the waves of the Dornoch Firth in the east. They helped drag farmers' cows out of flooding burns and clear fallen trees from storm-lashed roads. Through it all, Dorothy was the prettiest thing Hamish had ever seen in a Police Scotland rain jacket.

Summer's late departure led to an angry, impatient autumn that brought high winds and violent storms. Then, just as summer had been reluctant to leave, so winter arrived early with the first flurries of snow falling towards the middle of November. Sutherland then settled into a period of intense cold and the daylight hours dwindled, yet when the clouds cleared the sky was an intense steely blue. It was on one such day in mid-December that Hamish and Dorothy took a lunchtime stroll along the Lochdubh waterfront. The gulls wheeled and screeched above the choppy waters of the loch and the two police officers paused to take in the view. Although it had cleared elsewhere, the mountain-tops were still regally resplendent in a white crown of icy snow.

"I need to take some leave, Hamish," said Dorothy, "if that's okay with you."

"Is something wrong?" he asked.

"No, nothing wrong." She gave him a reassuring smile. "I have a lot of leave due and I need to go back down south. I have a flat that I need to sort out and other things to take care of if I'm to move up here permanently."

"How long do you need?"

"Three weeks. I'll be back in early January."

"If that's what you need, then it's fine by me." He tried to keep the note of dejection out of his voice but was pretty sure he failed.

She left at the end of that week, and, watching her car cross the humpbacked bridge, heading for the outside world, it suddenly seemed as though a great weight was pressing down on Hamish's shoulders. He had never felt so alone in all his life.

Hamish's great comfort while Dorothy was gone were his most loyal companions, Lugs and Sonsie. He was frying some venison sausages to share a breakfast with Lugs while Sonsie tucked into a dogfish he had defrosted from his freezer stock, when he finally made up his mind.

"I need to talk to you two about Dorothy," he said. Lugs wagged his tail at the mention of her name. Sonsie looked up from her fish and, Hamish was convinced, scowled at him. "You need to get used to having her around, Sonsie, because I have decided that as soon as she gets back, I'm asking her to marry me."

He waited for a reaction. There was none. Lugs had his eyes on the sausages in the pan and

Sonsie was concentrating on her fish. "That's settled then," he said, "but keep it under your hats for now. I know, you don't wear hats, but keep it to yourselves anyway."

Hamish gratefully floated through a series of generous invitations to Christmas and New Year parties on a high tide of excitement and nervousness about his decision, yet he told no one. He considered seeking Dorothy out in Glasgow and asking her straight away but he decided against it. The moment had to be special and it had to happen where they were going to spend the rest of their lives—Lochdubh. Dorothy called every other day to check in, the calls revolving around work, and it was all he could do not to blurt out a proposal through the telephone each time he heard her voice. She sounded preoccupied and desperate to leave Glasgow behind, which made him long to see her even more. When she finally did arrive back one evening a few days into the new year, a blizzard was raging.

"I wanted to let you know I'd made it back," she said, unzipping her snow-flecked parka in the warmth of Hamish's kitchen. She was wearing a colourful woollen sweater, dark blue ski pants, and fur-lined boots. "I . . . I missed you."

"Aye, we haff all chust missed you something terrible," Hamish admitted. The words were sticking in his throat. More than anything he wanted to throw his arms around her and tell her that he loved her but he felt awkward and unsure. Lugs was wrapping himself around Dorothy's legs. Sonsie sulked in a warm corner by the radiator. "Well, we all missed you except Sonsie. Would you like a coffee, or maybe a drink?"

"Thank you, but I won't stay. I need to unpack and get settled in again."

"I'll drive you . . ."

"No, my car is outside and I can manage fine in the snow, Hamish. I'll see you tomorrow."

The storm continued throughout the night, and although the wind had dropped by the time Dorothy trudged through the snow on foot to reach the station the following morning, large, heavy flakes were still falling. The loch was an unsettled grey and the mountains were obscured by the low cloud and the continuous barrage of white. Before long, the roads into the area were blocked and Lochdubh was cut off. Hamish and Dorothy telephoned outlying hamlets and isolated crofts to make sure that everyone was coping. Mr. Patel had stocked up on essentials in his shop to ensure he could keep his customers supplied, and whenever there was a break in the weather, Hamish and Dorothy battled alongside crofters in tractors and the snow ploughs from Strathbane to keep the main roads open.

After a few days, the snow suddenly stopped, the sky cleared, and the watery light of a late dawn gave way to a winter sun that turned the snow covering the fields and mountainsides into a white carpet scattered with a magical shimmer of countless diamond sparkles.

Dorothy was about to leave the hotel for the station when Hamish pulled up in his Land Rover.

"Jump in," he called. "Alice McBride's husband has gone missing and we need to have a wee look for him."

When the Land Rover broke out of the shaded avenue of rhododendrons on the hotel driveway, Dorothy pulled a pair of Ray-Bans from her pocket and slipped them on to protect her eyes from the intense glare of the sun on the snow.

"Are we starting the search at the McBrides' house?" she asked.

"No, I've a fair idea where he might be," said Hamish, heading out of the village and taking the road that ran along the northern edge of the loch. "McBride keeps a wee boat by a jetty way up on the north shore. We'll try there."

The road was deserted and alternated between hard-packed ice and soft drifts of windblown snow. Hamish maintained a careful, steady pace and the Land Rover took the road conditions in its stride.

"There's been a car down here before us," said Dorothy, pointing to fresh tyre tracks in the snow ahead.

"Aye, and there it is," Hamish replied, nodding towards the shore where a small van was parked near a finger of snow that stretched out a short way into the water. "He's been down at the jetty. Must be out on the water."

They rounded a bend and the loch opened out to a wide bay on its northern shore. In the middle of the bay, over a hundred yards from shore, was a dinghy with an outboard motor sitting silently on the calm water, a lone fisherman hunched over his rod.

"That's McBride all right." Hamish grinned. "Grabbed the first chance he got to get away from his wife and out on the loch for a bit of fishing."

Hamish phoned Alice McBride to let her know that her husband was safe, recoiling at the stream of vitriol when Alice vented her fury at her husband's wanton desertion. Abandoning the Land Rover, Hamish led Dorothy up the hillside to a flat vantage point where he produced a flask of hot coffee and spread his waterproof jacket on the snow. They sat close together.

"The view is absolutely amazing." Dorothy sighed, gazing out over the calm blue water and the pristine reflection of the dazzling white mountainside in the mirror of the loch.

"Aye . . . amazing," Hamish whispered, but when she turned to him she saw he was looking at her, not the loch. He leaned towards her, she drifted close to him, closed her eyes, and their lips met.

"This really won't do, Sergeant Macbeth," she breathed. "Two police officers kissing in public."

"There's no public. Just us two here together."

She thrust her fingers into his red hair and drew his face to hers, kissing him again. When he pulled away, he looked down into her blue eyes and said softly: "And this is how it should always be—you and me, the two of us, together. I love you, Dorothy—will you marry me?"

Reaching into his pocket, he produced a black velvet box.

"Hamish Macbeth!" she squealed. "I thought you'd never ask!" She threw herself at him and they tumbled backwards into the snow.

"Careful!" he laughed. "Don't lose the ring!"

She kissed him again, slowly, then they sat up and he carefully opened the box. The diamond flashed in the sunlight. She took the ring from its box and placed it on her finger. When she looked up at him, a tear rolled down her cheek.

"Dorothy, whateffer's wrong?"

"Nothing, you big eejit." She buried her face in his chest. "I've never been more happy in all my life."

CHAPTER THREE

*It's only in love and in murder that we
still remain sincere.*
               Friedrich Dürrenmatt

"He's dead! He's dead!" Dougie Tennant was squatting on the ground near his petrol pumps, rocking back and forth.

Hamish moved to Dougie's side and folded his lanky frame to kneel on one knee beside his friend. "Calm down now, Dougie. What's going on here? Who's dead?"

"In the car!" Dougie wailed. "Dead!"

"Don't worry, Dougie." Hamish stood slowly, patting Dougie on the shoulder. "We're here now. You're safe. Everything's going to be fine."

Hamish looked over at Dorothy, then nodded

towards Dougie. She took his place beside the distraught mechanic, speaking slowly and quietly, soothing and calming him. Leaving Dorothy to deal with Dougie, Hamish walked round the back of the car and approached the driver's door. In the wing mirror he could just make out the shape of a shoulder—a figure lying across the front seats. He took a quick, cautious glance through the open window, then instinctively ducked back out of harm's way. Then he relaxed. No harm was going to come from the man lying inside the car. Dougie was right: He was dead—the neat bullet hole in the side of his head said so. Although he couldn't actually see it, Hamish knew that the exit wound on the other side of the head would be far from neat. The splatter of blood and gore on the passenger seat and in the footwell was testament to that. Yet he needed to confirm that there really were no signs of life. He reached in and felt for a pulse. There was none.

Why did this have to happen now? He had been having a grand day. The sun was shining. The spring was promising some fine weather. He was about to get married, for heaven's sake! The last thing he wanted to be dealing with was a murder.

The heavy squad would be up from Strathbane, maybe even from Glasgow, blundering around and upsetting the locals. This was a disaster. Aye, he thought to himself, and not so good for the poor devil in the car, either. What was he doing here in the Highlands? And what had he done to make someone want to murder him?

The previous day had started out blissfully, with murder the farthest thing from Hamish's mind. He and Dorothy had paid a brief visit to the church for yet another chat with the minister, Mr. Wellington, who seemed more determined than anyone else that everything should be absolutely right for their big day. He regarded this as the most important wedding he had ever conducted in Lochdubh.

This meeting had been the most recent of several since they had first approached him the morning after they became engaged. On that day, they had met with both the minister and his wife, and Dorothy had been concerned about how to let everyone know they were engaged.

"That's not something you need worry about at all," the minister said with a smile.

"You have walked into the manse together in

your civilian clothes, and you wearing his ring," Mrs. Wellington noted. "If I am any judge of the way that tongues wag around here—and I am— the whole village will know by the time you get back to the station."

Just as Mrs. Wellington had predicted, word spread like wildfire, sending the residents of Lochdubh scurrying to cupboards and attic spaces to locate and dust off the toasters, wine glasses, serving dishes, and ceramic leaping-salmon orna- ments that had been returned after Hamish had called off his previous engagement. There were those who shook their heads sagely and issued dire predictions about what a challenge this new lassie would be for Hamish. She had expensive tastes, did she not? She liked fancy clothes, fancy food, fancy wine, and all of her creature comforts. Mrs. Mackenzie's place hadn't been good enough for her, had it? When she saw Tommel Castle, she had to stay there. There's no way she would ever end up living with Hamish in the draughty old police station. She'd be wanting something far better than that once they were married. She might look like butter wouldn't melt in her mouth, but there was another side to Macbeth's new fiancée. So went the endless rounds of gossip, dismissed out of hand by a buoyant Hamish whenever he heard whispers, his starry eyes now looking with undiluted optimism towards a blissful future with his beloved Dorothy.

The winter snow slowly thawed and soon the only patches of white to be seen by the roadside were not the last crusty remains of lingering snowdrifts but rather the delicate petals of wood anemones and cuckoo flowers. Then came the bluebells, and Hamish pointed out a crowd of their nodding sapphire caps near the base of the Faraway Tree as he and Dorothy walked back to the station after their latest visit to Mr. Wellington.

"There's some around here call them 'the fairy flowers,'" he said. "Sometimes the bells grow in white, and they say it's because a fairy has been visiting."

"You don't believe any of that old nonsense, do you?" Dorothy giggled.

"Not me, but there's plenty as do. It pays to give them that believe in fairies, ghosts, and witches a wee bit of respect, though. Not all of them are completely bonkers."

Hamish changed into his uniform at the station, then drove Dorothy to Tommel Castle to do likewise, before they set off to talk to a shop-keeper in Braikie about an attempted break-in. Leaving Lugs and Sonsie in the back of the Land Rover, Hamish chatted to Silas while Dorothy was getting changed.

"We have two guests at the moment who are a wee bit strange," said Silas. "Not like most of our usual clients at all."

"What have they been up to?"

"Nothing as far as I can tell, but you should check them out. They're in the car park."

Hamish walked outside and saw the two men standing together. One was tall, dark-haired, and slim, neatly dressed in a sweater and jeans. The other was shorter, heavily muscled, with a shaved head. He was wearing a black bomber jacket and sweat pants. Gold hung like anchor chains around his neck. Both men were holding handfuls of cash, and the taller one was swig-ging from a bottle of Coke.

"When I see two men in a car park counting cash," said Hamish, walking towards them, "it aye makes me a bit suspicious."

"This is none of your business," the thickset man sneered at Hamish. He had the guttural growl of a Glasgow accent. "Keep yer nose oot."

Hamish met the man's stare without flinching.

"I didn't much like the look of you before," he said, "and I like it a deal less now."

"Take it easy, guys." The other man had a relaxed American drawl. "There's nothing going on here, Officer—just a little wager between two friends."

Hamish looked at the two cars beside which the men were standing. The closer one was a silver Aston Martin. The farther one was a large yellow sports car of a make that he didn't recognise.

"Aye, just a wee bet," the Glaswegian smirked. "More than your week's wages, though. We need an honest man to hold the pot. Care to help us oot, Sergeant?"

"The bet's off," said Hamish. "Put your money away. If either of you tries racing round any part of the North Coast Five Hundred in either of these cars, I will get to know about it in less time than it takes you to fill your tanks. I will then come after you and that will not end well for you. Do you understand?"

"You listen to me, you jumped-up teuchter," snarled the Glaswegian. "We can do—"

"Wow!" Dorothy, now in uniform, approached the men. "Aston DB11. Nice. This one has the Mercedes vee-eight engine, right?"

"That's right." The American smiled. "A little down on power compared to its vee-twelve big brother, but it's a lot lighter. You sure know your cars, young lady."

"Och, I've always loved . . ." She paused, catching sight of the Glaswegian and frowning. He flashed a gold tooth in a vicious grin.

"Stick to the speed limits on our roads," Hamish warned the two men, "and we can all stay friends. Enjoy touring Sutherland, gentlemen. Come along, Constable."

They climbed into the Land Rover and Hamish started the engine.

"Did you know him?" he asked.

"Which one?"

"The bald one. You looked at him a bit funny."

"Never seen him before in my life." Hamish sensed a hint of a lie. "He looked really mean and ugly. Scary. I didn't like the way that he was talking to you."

Was that it? Hamish thought to himself. Was that what I heard in her tone? Was she just a wee bit feared? Concerned for me? He shook his head to clear his mind.

"I can handle thugs like him," Hamish said. "The American is different. Something odd about him. Get the licence numbers of those cars and call them in to headquarters. Let's find out who these two are."

"I'll talk to Silas as well," she said, reaching for the radio. "See if they checked in with their real names. Dorothy here, Alex. I need a check on a yellow Ford Mustang . . ."

Alex called back just as they arrived in Braikie. Leaving Dorothy to note down the information from Alex, Hamish went to talk to the shop-keeper. He was gone only a few minutes.

"Not much we can do here," he said, climbing back into the Land Rover. "Looks like somebody tried to prise open a rear window. Hoping to find a wee bit of cash, no doubt, but they didn't get in. I've told the manager and his neighbours to take extra care locking up and keep an eye out for any strangers lurking near their shops."

"Want to hear about our friends at the Tommel Castle?" Dorothy asked, waving her notebook.

"Aye, but there's a wee spot out by the coast where we can let the beasts out for a run around while we have a chat."

Hamish drove to Laxford Bay, where the Atlantic waters meandered inland from the sea loch to mingle with the fresh water from Loch

Stack and the larger Loch More. They parked just off the road by a small pier and released Lugs and Sonsie. The dog bounded off across the stony beach to plunge into the water. Sonsie sat on a sun-warmed boulder and stared out across the loch to the rocks opposite, where jet-black cormorants stretched their wings, posing like carved coal statues.

"There's some as thinks it a bit bleak here," said Hamish, gazing across the rough moorland that tumbled down to the rocky shoreline, "but when the sun's on the water, I like it just fine. Good fishing here and on the lochs up the river, too—salmon, sea trout, and char."

"It's beautiful, Hamish," Dorothy said, slipping her arm in his as they walked down to take a seat on the pier. "Alex told me that the Aston Martin was recently bought by James Bland, the American. The vulgar yellow Mustang is registered to a company in Glasgow that leases and services gaming machines."

"That's as may be," said Hamish, "but I didn't come here to talk about that."

"So what's on your mind?"

"The wedding. You've said nothing about who you will want to invite."

Dorothy looked down at the water. Her shoulders dropped and Hamish could see tears welling in her blue eyes.

"What's up with you?" he said gently, stretching a long arm around her and drawing her close. "There's no need for tears."

"I'm not like you, Hamish," she said, looking up at him, a tear staining her pale cheek. "You have three brothers, three sisters, and enough uncles, aunts, and cousins to fill a football ground. I have no one . . . only you."

"What about friends from down south?"

"I came here to see if I could start a new life, away from any so-called friends I might have had before. I never expected I'd end up wanting all of this so badly. I never expected to fall in love. Now all I want is a life here with you. I love you, Hamish."

She reached up and kissed him. He held her tight.

"If that's what you want," he said eventually, "then we needn't have such a big wedding."

Secretly, Hamish felt enormously relieved. Having been through all the angst of planning a wedding before, he was more than happy to keep things simple this time. They would have their

friends from the village, a couple of police colleagues, and keep it to that. Neither wild horses,
raging floods, nor rampant pestilence could hold
his mother back, though. She would make the
trip from Rogart but the rest of his family
would gladly forgo the expense of wedding gifts
and the cost of travelling to Lochdubh. Hamish
knew that, for them, family matters were important, but financial matters were paramount. By
keeping everything low-key, they would be doing
everyone a favour.

The following morning, Hamish and Dorothy
visited an isolated croft near Kylestrome where
an elderly gentleman called McTaggart lived. His
daughter had phoned Hamish from her home
far to the south in Hawick, worried because she
hadn't been able to get hold of her eighty-three-
year-old father by phone. They drove up the
track to the crofter's cottage, parking on a rough
patch of ground a few yards from the front door.
Hamish had just raised his hand to knock when
the door was flung open.

"Whit do you want?" A white-bearded, broad-
shouldered man wearing a heavy, slightly tattered,
green woollen sweater stood in the doorway.

"Mr. McTaggart?" said Hamish. "We had a call from your daughter in Hawick. She was worried that she couldn't get in touch with you."

"Aye, I'll bet she was," said the old man. "Phone's broke."

"Is it just not working?" asked Dorothy.

"Nope—it's broke." He reached out to a side-board and held up a clear plastic bag filled with the smashed remnants of a smartphone.

"That's broke, right enough," said Hamish. "How did that happen?"

"It happened wi' this," said the old man, reaching behind the door to produce a solid wooden cromach walking staff with a gnarled and bulbous head. "Now maybe she'll give me some peace and stop pestering the life out of me to go live wi' her down south in England."

"Hawick is in Scotland, sir, not England," Dorothy pointed out.

"It's not in my Scotland, lassie," the old man said. "Now I thank you for your trouble but I have to tend my sheep up on the hill. Come by, Brock!" A black-and-white sheepdog darted out of the door, which the old man closed but did not lock, before striding off up a path at the side of the cottage.

"Well, we can let that woman in Hawick know her father is in good shape." Hamish grinned, his keen hazel eyes tracking the old man making his way up the hillside.

"Certainly in better shape than his phone," Dorothy said with a laugh.

They were part way down the track when they heard the rumble of a potent engine, and the yellow Mustang thundered past on the main road, swiftly disappearing round a bend. Hamish grabbed his phone.

"Dougie, we've another customer for you . . ."

He was about to pull out onto the road when the rattle of the Land Rover's motor was drowned out by the howl of another vehicle, and a power-ful motorbike appeared. Hamish slammed on the brakes and the motorbike flashed past, its rider clad in black leather and crouched in a racing pose, upper body low over the fuel tank. They had no chance of identifying the rider, who was wearing a black, full-face helmet with a black visor, or even telling whether it was male or female. Hamish revved the Land Rover and set off in pursuit.

"They're going to kill themselves!" Hamish grimaced.

"Or someone else," Dorothy replied, switching on the Land Rover's siren and flashing blue lights.

Having lost track of the motorbike on a winding section of road, they spotted it in the distance in time to see a deer leap out from a copse of trees straight into its path. The rider swerved to avoid the animal and lost control, parting company with the bike. The motorcycle slid along the road on its side, metal scraping against the ground and throwing out a trail of sparks. The rider also slid along the road before crashing into the stands of bracken lining the roadside and slithering into a ditch out of sight.

"I'll go find him," said Hamish, closing on the crash site. "You grab the first-aid kit in the back."

Hamish didn't have to look far. No sooner had the Land Rover slithered to a halt than the rider appeared from the ditch, scuttling towards the motorbike. Hamish yelled at the rider to stay right there but the black-clad figure took one look at the big police sergeant, leapt the ditch, and bounded off up the hillside through the bracken and heather.

"There's a track round the back of this hill!"

Hamish shouted to Dorothy. "Take the car round to cut him off. I'll get after him."

A champion hill runner, Hamish was not only confident that he could catch up with the rider, but eager to show off his athleticism in front of Dorothy. Had he not won the cash prize at the Strathbiggie Games hill run, and many more before that? She would be mightily impressed with the way her future husband caught up with the man in black. It was, Hamish decided, a man. The way he moved, the way he ran, convinced him of that. He could see the black figure up ahead, still wearing the crash helmet and with a small black rucksack on his back.

With no real path to follow, it was tough going trying to move quickly through heather that was at times more than knee-high. Hamish was pushing hard, the swish of the heather against his legs almost drowned out by the sound of his laboured breathing and the hammering of his heart. He looked up to see the rider crest a rise and disappear from view. He redoubled his efforts and reached the crest only to find it was a false summit—a faint path led up through the heather to a higher hilltop. There was no sign of the rider. Hands on hips, sucking in air, Hamish scanned the hillside. Surely he couldn't have made it all the way up that path and over the other side? And wearing a helmet and rucksack? There was only one way to find out. Hamish dashed into the shallow depression before hitting the path and pounding to the top of the hill.

He stopped at the top, bending over with his hands on his knees, then straightening up with his hands behind his head, filling his lungs for whatever exertion might come next and sweeping the hillside with his eyes, searching for his quarry. He could see all the way down to the track where he had sent Dorothy, yet there was no sign either of her or the rider. Then he heard it—the sound of the motorbike engine starting up. He turned to look back down towards the road, immediately spotting the black-clad figure astride the motorbike. The rider gunned the engine and was gone.

Hamish was furious with himself. How could I have missed him? I must have run right past him! While I was charging all the way up here, all he had to do was trot back to the road! He's made me look like a complete bloody numpty! Cursing between breaths, he made his way down as fast as he could. He jogged along the road and passed the track but saw no sign of Dorothy. Rounding the next bend, he immediately spotted her sitting beside the Land Rover holding a cloth to her head. He sprinted over to her.

"Are you okay? What happened?" It was only then that he realised the Land Rover was leaning over at a crazy angle with two wheels in the roadside ditch.

"I drove past the track. I was turning the car round to head back when the motorbike came out of nowhere. I swerved and ended up in the ditch. Bashed my head on the side window." She took the cloth away, showed him the lump on the side of her forehead, then poured bottled water on the cloth to cool it, holding it against her head to stem the swelling. "Just as well I didn't cut it. Head wounds bleed like the devil. Makes them look a lot worse than they are."

"We need to get you home to Lochdubh," he said, helping her to her feet.

"No, Dougie will be waiting. Let's get this thing back on the road."

Using the winch on the front of the Land Rover and wrapping its cable around a giant boulder on the other side of the road, the car was quickly dragged out of the ditch. It had suffered no serious damage and within minutes they were speeding towards Dougie Tennant's filling station.

"You sure you're okay?" Hamish asked again.

"It's just a wee bump, Hamish. Don't fuss. How did that guy get back down to his bike?"

"No idea. Look, there's the Mustang by the pumps and . . . there's Dougie. Crivens! Something's not right here, Dorothy!"

"He's dead! He's dead!" Dougie Tennant chanted his mantra over and over again.

Hamish walked over to where Dorothy knelt beside Dougie. The mechanic was calming down, but it was clear he was still hugely distressed.

"We need to get him a good strong cup of sweet tea for the shock," he said.

"I want to see inside the car first," she said, standing.

"It's not very nice," he warned, clutching her arm to hold her back. She shook herself free.

"I've seen dead bodies before, Sergeant!" Approaching the car, she stared in through the driver's window where the bulky body of the shaven-headed man was sprawled sideways, the gold chains around his neck gleaming in a pool of blood on the passenger seat. Her jaw set and her eyes grew cold. "That's Graham Leslie, according to the Tommel Castle's register. That's what Silas told me."

"Let's have a wee look, then," said Hamish, pulling on a pair of gloves and opening the car door.

"Don't touch anything, Hamish. The forensic team will go nuts."

"He's been shot in the head. Not just killed. Not just murdered—assassinated. If someone's going to get himself assassinated on my patch, then I damn well want to know who he is."

Hamish slipped a hand inside the man's jacket and retrieved a wallet from which he produced a photocard driver's licence.

"Graham Leslie, right enough," he said, "but who is he and what is he doing here? I'll call this in and get the team up from Strathbane, Dorothy. You get Dougie inside for that tea."

Within an hour a convoy of police vehicles had arrived and filled the forecourt of Dougie Tennant's petrol station, blue lights flashing. They parked well clear of the blue-and-white striped police tape that Hamish and Dorothy had strung around the crime scene. Hamish spoke with a sergeant whom he knew from Strathbane.

"Tell them to switch off the lights, Kenny," he said. "There's no need for that—and what's that thing doing here?" He pointed to a large white police van with MAJOR INCIDENT COMMAND UNIT emblazoned on the side.

"Orders from on high." The sergeant nodded towards an approaching car. "Ask him yourself."

The car drew to a halt and the wiry figure of Detective Chief Inspector Jimmy Anderson stepped out. Hamish and Jimmy were old friends, but instead of Jimmy's normal cheery greeting, Hamish was met with a dark, sombre expression. Combined with his dark suit, it gave Jimmy the look of a funeral director. He motioned for Hamish to step away from the other officers.

"What's going on, Jimmy? It's a murder right enough, and none more serious, but this is a hell of a turnout."

"I'll explain later, Hamish. You need to let the forensics boys and the pathologist do their stuff. Best if you head back to Lochdubh."

"You're not taking me off the case, are you, Jimmy? This is my patch. I spoke to the victim only yesterday. I got Dougie to delay him here. I—"

"I know all that, laddie." Jimmy recognised the rising anger in Hamish's voice and gestured for him to calm down, pushing gently with his hands as though against an invisible wall. "Just keep your heid and we'll talk about this later. I'll be there as quick as I can. Take her with you."

"Make sure they look after Dougie—he's not used to this sort of thing. He's in shock. He's not been able to tell us anything."

Dorothy was walking towards them. Hamish headed for the car.

"With me, Constable!"

She heard him coming up the stairs. There was no mistaking the lethargic stomp of his footsteps, no mistaking the bellowing voice, no mistaking the rage, no mistaking the foul language. For some reason, Mary Blair's husband was home early from work.

"No, it's you that doesn't understand!" Mary heard him ranting into his phone. "It would be way more suspicious if I refused. I can't refuse—it's orders. Ach . . . phone me later!"

Mary was standing in the open doorway of

their flat, arms folded, leaning against the door-post, when he arrived, puffing with exertion, at the top of the stairs.

"Keep your voice down," she hissed. "What will the neighbours think?"

"Bollocks to the neighbours!" he roared.

"What are you doing home at this hour?"

"Need to pack a bag," he grunted, pushing past her. "Got to go away for a few days."

"What's all this about?" she asked, following him into the flat. "Where are you going?"

"There's been a murder," he said. "They're putting together a special team and they want me on it because of my contacts."

"But that's a good thing, isn't it?"

"A 'good thing'? Have you lost the plot completely, woman? How can you be so stupid? A 'good thing' is what I was starting to get going here in Glasgow. That's all shot to pieces if I'm not right here on the spot!"

"So where are they sending you?"

"Lochdubh! Bloody Lochdubh!"

It was almost noon when Jimmy Anderson's driver delivered him to the police station at Lochdubh. The DCI strode into the kitchen, dropped a briefcase on the floor, flopped into a chair, and said, "Where's the hooch?"

"Bit early, is it not?" said Hamish, knowing full well what Jimmy's response would be.

"Rubbish, laddie! The sun's yards past the yardarm," said Jimmy, reciting one of his favourite catchphrases, "and it's already . . ."

"I know, I know," Hamish interrupted him, "already pooping on the poop deck. That doesn't change the fact that I've no whisky."

"Well get some," ordered Jimmy. "My throat's as dry as a witch's . . . ah . . . hello, dear."

Dorothy walked through from the office. "Good morning, sir."

"Constable," said Jimmy, fishing in his wallet to retrieve a few notes. "I've had a very long night and an even longer morning. Pop down to the shop and pick us up a bottle, there's a good lass."

Dorothy looked at Hamish, who nodded, then she took the notes. "Of course, sir. I'll be back shortly."

"She's a real stunner, eh, Hamish?" said Jimmy once Dorothy was out of earshot. "I'm not surprised you fell for her charms. Something about a woman in uniform that puts lead in your pencil, eh?"

"Don't talk about Dorothy like that," Hamish warned, ignoring the fact that Jimmy was his superior officer, "and don't ever use her like some sort of message girl. She's a police officer, not your skivvy."

"Okay, point taken," said Jimmy defensively. "I'll make it up to her. I'm right pleased for you about the engagement, laddie, honestly. I'll be pleased to toast your future happiness together . . . as soon as she gets back wi' the good stuff."

"So what's going on with this shooting?" Hamish asked. "Kenny Stewart said there had been 'orders from on high.' Are you not in charge of the investigation?"

"Yes and no. We have our own Major Investigation Team in Strathbane and we spent last night on a raid to tie up a drugs bust that we've been on for months. It's not all exactly cut and dried yet, and sorting out the evidence and the loose ends will take even longer, and we're short on manpower anyway, and . . ."

"They're bringing in another team."

"Aye, but there's more to it than that."

Dorothy arrived back at that moment and

placed a bottle of Glenmorangie on the table. Jimmy stood and drew back a chair for her.

"Would you join us, please, Constable?" he said smoothly. "This will involve you as well."

Hamish got each of them a glass and Jimmy poured generous measures.

"First of all"—he raised his glass—"congratulations to the both of you. I wish you the very best." They clinked glasses. "Now to business."

Jimmy retrieved his briefcase from the floor and pulled out a beige file, which he opened on the table in front of Hamish and Dorothy.

"Your victim was Graham Leslie, a right nasty piece of work. He has a string of convictions for theft, extortion, assault, you name it. He's spent half his adult life behind bars."

"There's plenty of folk in here that would want him dead," said Hamish as they flicked through the file.

"No doubt," Jimmy agreed, refilling his glass, "and plenty not in here, I should think. I'm waiting for more information on him." He offered the bottle to Hamish and Dorothy. They both declined, having barely touched their drinks.

"He was involved with the Macgregor crime

family in Glasgow," said Dorothy, looking up from the notes.

"He was," Jimmy confirmed. "They used him as an enforcer, a bodyguard, and a debt collector— the kind that breaks your legs wi' an iron bar if you don't pay up on time. His connection wi' organised crime is the main reason why they're sending the big boys up from Glasgow."

"But what was he doing here?" said Hamish. "This is not the kind of place for a thug like that. There's nobody around here for him to show off to in his fancy yellow Mustang. Cruising the streets in a big city is way different from cruising through Lochdubh."

"He was racing on the North Coast Five Hundred," Dorothy pointed out.

"Not really his scene, though, is it?" said Hamish. "He wasn't really the type. He was a flashy thug. You can't be flashy when there's nobody watching you being flashy. So why was he here?"

"That's what I need you working on," said Jimmy. "We need to know if he was setting up something for the Macgregors and who else was involved. We've enough problems without letting big-city turf wars spill over into our territory."

"The team from Glasgow will have their work

cut out tracking down all of the potential suspects from Leslie's past," said Dorothy. "They'll
not get far with that here in Lochdubh. They'll
need to be in the city."

"Aye," Hamish agreed, reading Leslie's arrest
record, "and it seems he's been up to no good over
the years in Edinburgh, Dundee, and Aberdeen
as well."

"Whenever the Macgregors have been looking
to expand their business over the past twenty-
five years," Jimmy explained, "Leslie was the
first one they sent to show any local mob that
they were not to be messed with."

"That means the Glasgow team will have to
cast their net even wider," Dorothy said.

"And they'll have less time to spend around
here," said Jimmy, "which gives us an advantage.
So what do we really know about what happened?
Did yon mechanic tell you anything?"

"Dougie didn't see a thing," said Dorothy.
"He was in the back room of the petrol station
listening to Biffy Clyro on his headphones."

"One of his favourites," Hamish mused. "Them
and Runrig."

He looked up from the notes and watched
Jimmy gulp down another swig of Glenmorangie.

Jimmy returned his stare, bloodshot blue eyes unblinking in his foxy face, then reached for the bottle again. Hamish knew there was something that Jimmy wasn't telling them.

"Does Superintendent Daviot know you're talking to us?" he asked. "I'm guessing the drugs case isn't going well, is it?"

"That's not your concern!" Jimmy snapped. "I know what you're like, Hamish Macbeth. We've known each other for long enough. Officially, I'm here to tell you to stay well clear of this murder enquiry . . ."

"But unofficially you want us to find out who killed Graham Leslie so that you can take the credit for it and be in Daviot's good books, just in case the big drugs case blows up in your face and leaves you looking like a total dunderheid," said Hamish.

"I won't deny that it would look good for me," said Jimmy. "Daviot is piling the pressure on and I need that kind of result right now. It will be good for you, too, though, because as long as we stay friends, I can turn a blind eye to you two lovebirds working together. By rights I should be insisting that one of you is transferred out of here, but I don't want to do that."

"Is that a threat, Jimmy?" said Hamish, bristling.

"Not at all, laddie. We both want this murder cleared up. I'll give you all the help I can and anything that you find out will be passed on to the Glasgow team—but it comes to me first."

"We can do that," said Dorothy quickly, "can't we, Hamish?"

"Aye," Hamish agreed, seeing the look of concern on her face, "we can do that, Jimmy."

"So what have you got so far? Anything from the hotel?"

"Not really." Hamish shook his head. "There's one character there, an American by the name of Bland, who's a bit suspicious. I'll have a word with him before the Glasgow boys get to him."

"And there's the motorbike," said Dorothy, opening her notebook. "Reported stolen yesterday in Dundee by the owner, Keith Bain. It looked like Leslie was racing against it when we first saw them out on the road."

"But it could have been chasing him," Hamish added, and he related the story of their encounter with the black-clad rider.

"An assassin on a motorbike?" Jimmy mused. "Sounds like a good place to start. Track down the bike and the rider but keep it to yourselves for now. No need for any mention of the motor-bike in your reports."

"The Glasgow team will find out about it eventually," Hamish reasoned, looking at Dorothy. "We'll have to say we thought it was an unrelated speeding incident."

"We need to get up to the hotel to speak to Bland," said Dorothy, looking at her watch, "before anyone else does."

"Right you are." Jimmy drained his glass. "And when's your stag night, Hamish? I wouldn't want to miss that."

"I haven't really thought about that," Hamish admitted.

"Then we'll think about it for you." Jimmy smiled for the first time since he had walked into the station. "I'll talk to Silas and we'll sort it out."

"It's a good idea, Hamish," said Dorothy, squeezing his hand. "You should get your friends here involved with the wedding."

"Oh, and there's one last thing," said Jimmy, taking a step towards the door. "Blair is part of the Glasgow team."

Hamish sighed and shook his head. There, at

last, was the real reason that Jimmy wanted them to conduct their own investigation. Jimmy had taken Blair's job when Daviot banished Blair to Glasgow. For years previously, Blair had managed to maintain a hold over Daviot—with compromising photographs of his wife, taken when she had been drugged—but Hamish had recovered the photos, and then when Blair's behaviour had become intolerable, Daviot had gotten rid of him. The last thing Jimmy wanted was for Blair to return like some kind of deranged, vengeful, prodigal son, find some new way to manipulate Daviot and be welcomed back to Strathbane. Yet how likely was that, really? Would Blair even want to come back to Strathbane? Hamish certainly didn't want the scunner anywhere near his patch. Maybe he should have a word with Mary. That might shed some light on it all.

In the meantime, he and Dorothy had to be on the lookout for whatever trouble might come their way, and in Hamish's experience, the worst trouble always came in the form of one man—Blair!

CHAPTER FOUR

*As iron is eaten away by rust, so the envious
are consumed by their own passion.*
Antisthenes

"I am *not* a murderer." James Bland maintained his composure for the most part, but there was no doubting the irritation in his voice.

"I'm not accusing you of murder, Mr. Bland," Hamish assured him. "I just need to know where you were this morning so that I can eliminate you from our enquiries."

"I don't want to get caught up in your investigation, Sergeant Macbeth. I got a lot of things I want to do while I'm here in Scotland."

"Ah, yes, sir, and what might those things

be? What is it that you're doing up here in Sutherland?"

Bland looked from Hamish to Dorothy, seemed to realise that he wasn't about to walk away from this situation as quickly as he had hoped, and relaxed against his Aston Martin. Hamish and Dorothy had pulled up alongside him in the Tommel Castle car park just as he had stepped out of the car. He folded his arms across his chest, his dark eyes studying them from beneath even darker, heavy brows.

"I'm a tourist, Sergeant," he explained, "just like any other."

"Not quite like any other," Dorothy commented. "Most tourists arrive in camper vans or family cars, not Aston Martins."

"I hired this for the duration of my stay in Scotland. It's for fun. I guess you might say I was fulfilling a kind of secret-agent fantasy. Me, James Bland, driving an Aston Martin like your James Bond drives an Aston Martin."

Dorothy looked at the ground to try to hide a giggle and Bland smiled.

"See? She gets it," he said. "Just a bit of fun."

"Och, I get it just fine, Mr. Bland"—Hamish

remained stony faced—"but you didn't answer my question: Where were you this morning?"

"I drove over to Skibo Castle."

"Where Madonna got married?" said Dorothy. "I've not been but I hear it's fantastic."

"It is," Bland agreed. "It's a cut above this place, that's for sure."

"Yet you chose to stay here," said Hamish. "Why not at Skibo?"

"I'm booked to stay at Skibo next week."

"Must be nice to have enough money to travel around, staying in lovely hotels." Dorothy sighed.

"That was a long drive just for you to see the hotel," said Hamish.

"Not such a long drive in this car," Bland replied, moving to the rear of the vehicle, "and I didn't go just to view the facilities. Take a look in the trunk."

He popped open the boot to reveal a set of golf clubs.

"I played Royal Dornoch yesterday," said Bland, "and the guy I played with there suggested a return match at Skibo—they sure are fine courses. It's an easy enough alibi to check, Sergeant."

"And you can be sure that I will be doing that, Mr. Bland. Where is it that you live exactly?"

"Glencoe."

"Really?" said Dorothy. "Glencoe isn't so far from here."

"I know." Bland laughed. "I'm just joshing with you. My Glencoe is in Cook County—Chicago. One of the reasons I came here was to see the original Glencoe."

"How long have you been over here?"

"A couple of weeks."

"When do you plan to go back to America?" asked Hamish.

"I'll be sticking around for a while yet."

"Please don't leave without checking in with us first, Mr. Bland."

"I won't," said Bland. "Can I go inside now? I've been looking forward to a drink ever since I left Skibo. I won a packet from the guy I was playing, so it's time to celebrate. Care to join me?"

"Thank you, but we have other things to do." Hamish climbed back into the Land Rover and started the engine. Dorothy settled into the passenger seat and he looked at her, a slight frown furrowing his brow. He wasn't best pleased that she had been giggling during their chat with

Bland, but when she turned towards him her face was deadly serious.

"He was lying," she said, and Hamish nodded.

"I thought so, too, but his alibi will be simple to check."

"He was lying about the car." She pulled her notebook from a pocket. "The car is not rented. He bought it from a specialist dealer in Edinburgh six weeks ago and he is the registered owner. He's been here far longer than 'a couple of weeks.' Silly things to lie about—easy for us to check. Why would he do that?"

"Sometimes people lie when they are caught off guard or are nervous. Perhaps he wasn't as relaxed as he seemed. We need to take a closer look at our Mr. Bland. There may be more to him than meets the eye. Wait here a minute, would you? I need to have a quick word with Silas."

Hamish found Silas at the back of the hotel, standing with Freddy in a patch of sunshine outside the kitchen. Both were eating bacon baps.

"Let me guess," said Hamish. "You've had a delivery from Dick and Anka."

"There's no fooling you." Freddy laughed, wiping a dusting of white flour from his mouth. "I've tried, but I can't make baps like they do."

"Best ever with a nice bit of bacon," Silas agreed between mouthfuls.

"I can rustle one up for you if you like," Freddy offered.

"Sadly, I've not got time," said Hamish. "I need to have a wee word about Dorothy. I want you two to watch out for her. Make sure she's okay."

"We'd do that anyway," Silas said. "Is there a problem?"

"I'm just worried about her," Hamish admitted. "First, there was that woman who came here. Now we've got this Bland character staying here and I don't trust him. Then there's the murder. We were right close by when it happened and the murderer might get to know that."

"Why would the murderer come after Dorothy?" asked Freddy.

"He might think that she saw something. He might think she could identify him," Hamish explained.

"But she can't, can she?" Silas argued. "And if he thought that about her, he'd likely think the same about you. Maybe you're worrying too much, Hamish. And anyway, she's a police officer, and . . ."

"Just humour me, will you? We're getting married on Saturday."

"Aye, no problem," said Silas. "Last thing at night, I'll double-check everything's locked up tight and do a final prowl of the corridors."

"And my room's in the attic right above Dorothy's," Freddy reassured Hamish. "I'm a light sleeper. Usually up around five in the morning. I'll hear if anything happens."

"Thanks, lads." Hamish walked quickly back to the Land Rover.

Having returned to the police station to a rapturous welcome from Lugs and what had become Sonsie's customary greeting—purrs and affection for Hamish and a cold rejection when Dorothy stooped to pat her—Hamish decided that a coffee would perk them up.

"Pay no heed to her, Dorothy." He was almost apologetic about the behaviour of the big wild cat. "She'll come round to you eventually. Now let's get the kettle on and set about these reports for Jimmy."

With Hamish busying himself in the kitchen, Dorothy gave Sonsie a hard, icy stare and whispered: "You're going to have to get used to me, puss—I'm here to stay." Sonsie bared her teeth and hissed.

"No point in trying too hard to make friends." Hamish was striding towards the office with two mugs of coffee. "Sonsie's not everybody's idea of a pet."

They sat back to back at desks in the small office at the front of the building, each typing on a laptop while Lugs lay dozing on the floor in a patch of sunlight that streamed in through the window. They had been working quietly for about half an hour when the bleep of Hamish's phone shattered the silence.

"Silas," said Hamish. "What can I do for you?"

"Thought you'd want to know that a bunch of detectives from Glasgow have just checked in, and there's a TV crew due this afternoon as well."

"Let me guess—Elspeth." Elspeth Grant was another that Hamish had asked to marry. A reporter and TV news presenter based in Glasgow, she was loath to be away from the big city and her career there for any length of time, but her local connections made her the first choice to cover any big stories in the north. Stories didn't come much bigger than a gangland assassination.

"Right first time. The hotel's full, the bar is

serving beer and whisky like it's Hogmanay, and the colonel is going nuts."

"I'd have thought he'd be pleased to have the business."

"Not with the tourist season kicking off, Hamish. He thinks this lot will scare everyone else away. He wants to know when they'll all be gone. I think you can expect a visit."

"Thanks for the warning, Silas. Is the American, Bland, still with you?"

"Aye, he's still here."

"Keep an eye on him for me, would you? Let me know if he tries to check out."

Silas rang off and Sonsie appeared, leaping into Hamish's lap.

"Get off, you daft cat," he scolded her affectionately. "And get your paws off my keyboard. Sure and you've just typed a load of cat nonsense."

He lifted Sonsie out of his lap and had no sooner lowered her to the floor than her place was taken by Dorothy. She put her arms around his neck and kissed him.

"No that I'm complaining," he said, "but what was that for?"

"Because I love you. Do I need any other reason?"

"None whatsoever," he assured her, and they kissed again, slowly, enjoying the closeness of their embrace.

"Who's Elspeth?"

"That's not a wee bit of jealousy I'm detecting, is it?"

"Och, you're such a fine detective, Hamish Macbeth," she said with a smile, her eyes bright with mischief. "I admit it—I confess! I am jealous of Sonsie and of Elspeth and of anyone else who gets your attention. I want you all to myself."

"Elspeth and I were . . . an item, once . . ."

"An 'item'?" Dorothy laughed. "That's an expression I've not heard in a long time. You don't have to feel embarrassed about it, Hamish. You're not her 'item' any more, after all—you're all mine."

She kissed him again and then pulled away abruptly.

"Oh, heavens," she said, leaping out of his lap. "We've been spotted."

Standing out in the street, at the wall of the small front garden, were the Currie twins. They were wearing their identical camel-hair coats, identical tweed hats, and identical expressions of horrified disapproval.

"I'd better go mollify them," she said, smiling and waving to the two women. "We don't want them thinking we're like this all day!"

Hamish watched her trotting up the short path to greet the women. She treated them to a huge smile. He felt his heart skip. Her happiness was contagious, and even the twins were not immune. Jessie and Nessie were soon smiling and nodding, Nessie saying a few words, Jessie providing the chorus. How did Dorothy manage that? How did she manage to win over those two old curmudgeons? It was like she had a kind of energy that she could share without even touching you—you could benefit just by being near her. Elspeth would have something to say about that. She came from a family gifted with the second sight, and she could see and sense things that others could not. Aye, he thought to himself, Elspeth will have plenty to say about Dorothy, right enough. He ran his fingers through his red hair and turned to his computer screen just as his phone rang again. It was Jimmy.

"The bike's turned up. It was abandoned at Lairg station. I need you to get there before the recovery truck and take a look at it. Soon as they know it exists, the Glasgow lot will be all over it."

"We can be there in an hour."

"Get going then, laddie! We need to stay one step ahead of these bampots."

With Hamish at the wheel of the Land Rover, he and Dorothy took the road heading south-west, where the inland hills lost some of the dramatic grandeur of their coastal cousins, turning to rolling moorland with slopes clad in green cloaks of forest pine. From time to time, the forests surrendered to stark grey wastelands of treeless devastation where the pines had been harvested, leaving behind hillsides that were blighted and traumatised by the havoc wreaked upon them. Such eyesores did not detract from the beauty of the countryside for more than a moment or two and were forgotten by the time they reached Oykel Bridge, where the hotel, much favoured by anglers, was the most notable building they had seen since leaving Lochdubh.

Their conversation ebbed and flowed and it seemed to Hamish as though the drone of the engine might be sending Dorothy to sleep. Then, as they approached Rosehall, she became suddenly more animated.

"Can you see? Over there on the other side of the river. You can just spot it through the trees."

Hamish glanced to the right, then back to the road. He could just make out a forlorn-looking old mansion.

"What exactly am I looking for?"

"That's Rosehall House, once owned by Hugh Grosvenor, the Duke of Westminster. In the 1920s he was one of the richest men in the world. One of his mistresses was Coco Chanel. He showered her with jewels, bought her land on the French Riviera, and he bought Rosehall House as one of their wee love nests. She decorated it with handprinted wallpaper to remind her of her apartment in Paris. Imagine being able to do that, Hamish. Imagine having . . . having all that money."

"Hard for me to imagine, really. I don't think I would know what to do with that much money."

"Well, I certainly would." She leaned back in her seat, frowning. "I would know just what to do with it. It's not fair that some people are that rich. Not fair at all."

Once through the Rosehall hamlet, they were within easy striking distance of Lairg. They crossed the River Shin and headed south to where the railway station lay a couple of miles outside the town. There they met Fergus Murray, the railway worker who had found the bike.

"This is the one all right," said Dorothy, looking at the licence plate.

"Aye, and the damage down the side is from where it slid along the road," Hamish agreed. "Amazing that it was still able to start up and go."

"It doesn't look like there's anything here that will tell us much about the rider."

"Except where it was found. Whoever dumped it here most likely caught the train out."

"Did you see who abandoned the bike here, Mr. Murray?"

"I didn't see anybody. Whit about the reward?" asked Murray.

"What reward?" said Dorothy.

"Surely there must be a reward for finding something as valuable as this," said Murray. "I mean, this bike must be worth a fair bit."

Hamish stuck his hand in his pocket and fished out a twenty-pound note.

"This is for being an honest citizen," he said, offering the note to Murray but then snatching it back just as Murray almost had his fingers on it. "But when the recovery truck arrives, or any other police officers ask, you tell them nothing about us having been here."

"That's a lot to ask for twenty quid," said Murray, raising an eyebrow to show he was in the mood to negotiate.

"It's either that or I tell your boss that you've been drinking on the job again," Hamish growled.

"How did you ken about that?" Murray gasped.

"I didn't"—Hamish smiled—"but I do now. So you hold your tongue about us being here, or I'll be making life very difficult for you."

Murray grabbed the note and wandered off, mumbling to himself. Hamish and Dorothy got back in the Land Rover and set off to retrace their route back to Lochdubh.

"It's a pity we didn't have time to check for CCTV images," Dorothy said. "There can't be many people who have caught trains out of here."

"Probably not," Hamish agreed, "but if our motorcycle assassin is canny enough to hide in the heather while I ran past without spotting him, he's no going to let himself be recognised on any CCTV they might have at Lairg station. Something doesn't feel right about this. We need to talk to the owner of that bike."

"Keith Bain," said Dorothy, consulting her notebook. "He's a twenty-year-old soldier in the Black Watch, stationed at Fort George in Ardersier."

"We'll need permission from the army to pay him a visit. It's not really on our patch, but see if you can contact the fort and get us in there to talk to Bain as soon as possible."

Hamish concentrated on the road while Dorothy called one number after another, eventually getting through to Bain's commanding officer. He tuned out of her conversation and ran through his futile pursuit of the leather-clad figure on the hillside. Judging by the way he had moved, bounding uphill through the heather, he must have been very fit. Could he have been a young soldier, used to yomping cross-country? A soldier would be trained to conceal himself. That would explain how Hamish had managed to miss him. Military training would also give him weapons skills—he would know how to shoot. Hamish shook his head, thinking to himself that you didn't need much skill to put a gun to someone's head and pull the trigger. And how might Bain be connected with a gangland thug like Leslie?

"Tomorrow morning, at nine-thirty," Dorothy said, shoving her phone back into her pocket. "We'll be meeting Captain Munro, Bain's CO."

"It will take us at least two hours to reach Inverness. We'll have to be on the road early."

"Not a problem. If you pick me up at the hotel, I'll be ready."

"Might it not be better...perhaps...if you just sort of...moved in with me? After all, we are about to be..."

"About to be married," she interrupted, smiling and squeezing his arm. "I hear you, Hamish Macbeth, but it's not that long until the big day, and I want our wedding night to be...special. You understand, don't you?"

"Aye, aye, of course," Hamish said, failing completely to disguise the ring of disappointment in his voice.

"I knew you would!" She reached over, grabbed his face in both hands, and kissed him. The car wobbled as his hands twitched the steering wheel.

"Careful!" He laughed. "You'll have the old Land Rover back in a ditch again!"

Outside the police station in Lochdubh, Colonel George Halburton-Smythe paced back and forth, muttering to himself. He was a small, neat man, dressed in an immaculate tweed jacket, a checked shirt with his tightly knotted regimental tie, sharply creased trousers, and highly polished brown brogues. He looked down at his shoes. He liked shoes. His father had made a fortune running a chain of high-street shoe shops, money that had allowed George to attend Eton and the Royal Military Academy at Sandhurst. As a young man he had quickly come to realise that having money allowed you to entertain lavishly, to rub shoulders with nobility, and to count aristocrats from society's top drawer among your acquaintances. He became acutely aware, however, that those who boasted ancestors who'd fought with Robert the Bruce at Bannockburn or who had served at the right hand of royalty for centuries did not regard him as their equal. His family money, after all, had been made through common commercial trade— not acquired, defended, preserved, and nurtured over centuries.

The colonel's most desperate desire had always been to be accepted in high society. It was what had led him to pursue and marry Philomena Halburton, the second daughter of a very well-regarded, if severely under-funded, family of landed gentry. He had thought that joining her name to his would be the magical key that unlocked the elusive portal to the sunlit uplands of lofty social status. He was wrong. Even buying Tommel Castle when he inherited his father's fortune hadn't really helped—and he'd nearly lost the lot when a bunch of swindling investment consultants had duped him out of most of his inheritance. It was Hamish Macbeth who had saved the day by suggesting that they turn the castle into a hotel.

"Where is that damned policeman?" he groaned. Then, for lack of anyone else to listen, he addressed the huge cat watching him from the garden wall. "I shouldn't have to wait around for the likes of him. What's that lazy scoundrel up to this time?"

Sonsie watched him dispassionately, enjoying the sun-soaked warmth of the stone wall. Lugs, snoozing on the doormat, raised an eyebrow and then an ear, prompting the colonel to look towards the bridge at the far end of the village, where the white police Land Rover duly appeared.

The colonel confronted Hamish as he stepped out of the car. "Where on earth have you been all afternoon?"

"Police business." Hamish shrugged. "Something I can help you with?"

"Yes, there is! You can send that bunch of layabouts at my hotel back where they came from!"

"Calm down now, sir," Dorothy soothed him. "Let's go inside for a chat. I'll get the kettle on."

Hamish and the colonel sat at the kitchen table while Dorothy served tea in steaming mugs and fussed over Lugs. The colonel watched her with an appraising eye. He could see what a fine-looking, charming young woman she was—that much had been clear from the first time he had seen her at the hotel.

"I don't think that I can get rid of the detectives," said Hamish, thanking Dorothy for the tea. "Most of them will outrank me, so I can't really tell them what to do."

"Maybe I should have a word with Peter Daviot," suggested the colonel. He and Philomena were on very good terms with Superintendent Daviot and his wife, Susan.

"I doubt there's much Mr. Daviot can do, either," Hamish advised, "except tell them to behave themselves, and I'm sure I can have a gentle word with them about that. In any case, they will be gone in a couple of days. It won't take them long to talk to all the locals and realise that they're wasting their time. This is a Glasgow gangland killing, not a local issue."

"Ah, yes, the murder." The colonel leaned forward, the glint of keen interest in his eye. "Anything I can do to help with that?"

"There just may be." Hamish also leaned forward, motioning the colonel to move even closer, as though turning their chat into a conspirators' plot. He knew that the colonel had always fancied himself an amateur detective. "See if you can listen in on what the detectives are saying. It would be good to know if they pick up any leads. And keep an eye on the American, Bland," he added, despite having told Silas to do exactly the same. "There's something not quite right about that lad."

"I see," mused the colonel, stroking his chin. "You think Bland may be the killer? You think he may be a hired hitman?"

"Anything's possible," said Dorothy. "He appears to have a sound alibi, but until we know more about him, we can't be sure he's not involved."

"I will do my utmost," the colonel assured them, sipping his tea. "You can rely on me."

The colonel, having walked to the station house seething with resentment towards the police, drove back to the hotel with Hamish and Dorothy, now imagining himself as a police special agent, excitedly propounding murder theories from the back seat. Hamish looked at Dorothy and saw the flicker of a smile. He winked.

"Hearts and minds," he whispered.

"Whit? No room? Do you know who I am?" There came a hoot of laughter from the bar area and DCI Blair shot a look of pure malice towards the sound, roaring at the detectives sitting there. "You lot watch yourselves or I'll have you all pounding the beat in Possilpark before you can say 'permanent night shift'!"

"Please keep your voice down, sir." Mr. Johnson, manager of the Tommel Castle Hotel, was behind the desk, having emerged from the office to take the receptionist's place when he heard

Blair's angry bluster. "There's no need to lose your temper."

"There's every need!" Blair howled, his chubby face purple with fury. "I've no desire to be out here in the back o' beyond dealing wi' a bunch of inbred teuchters, and now you tell me there's no room for me!"

"You should really have booked before you came." Silas, having heard the commotion, walked into the reception area. "The hotel is full, Mr. Blair."

"You!" Blair fixed Silas with a venomous stare. "I mind o' you. In times past you wouldn't dare look me in the eye. Well, don't you be so cocky, you wee shite! And it's 'Chief Inspector Blair' to the likes o' you."

"I am no longer a serving police officer, *Mister* Blair," said Silas, calmly returning Blair's stare, "and no longer work for you. Keep your voice down and mind your language or I will have to ask you to leave."

"Ask me to leave? And whit if I don't want to leave? Who's going to throw me out—you?"

"No," came Hamish's voice, "that would be me."

Blair turned to see Hamish walking through the front door. He took three strides towards

Blair before Dorothy hurried to his side, placing a cautionary hand on his shoulder.

"Well, well . . . I wondered when you would show yourself," Blair sneered, then flicked a dark look at Dorothy. "And this will be your latest squeeze, is it?"

Dorothy was about to speak when Hamish turned to face her.

"I will handle this, Constable," he said. They exchanged a look, he nodded, and she collected her room key from reception.

"So *she* has a room," growled Blair, watching Dorothy disappear up the main staircase before rounding on Mr. Johnson. "I'm the senior officer here. I'll take her room and she can move back into the station wi' lover boy."

"Constable McIver has neffer—*neffer*—stayed over at the station," said Hamish.

"Never stayed over?" Blair gave a rasping laugh. "You mean you've no slept wi' her? She wouldn't let you sample the goods before she got that ring on her finger?"

Hamish lunged towards Blair, but Silas, despite being the smallest of the three, quickly stepped between them, pushing Hamish back. "Let's not let this get out of hand," he said.

"Perhaps, Chief Inspector," said Mr. Johnson, "you might find a room at Mrs. Mackenzie's boardinghouse?"

"That'll be the day," grunted Blair. "I'm not staying at yon dosshouse. No—I outrank the sergeant here, so I think I will move into the station—and if he doesn't like it, he can drag his scrawny arse off to Mackenzie's hovel."

"That won't be necessary," said Silas. "I have a very comfortable room here—more like a small apartment, really—and I will put that at your disposal, Chief Inspector. That way you are here along with the rest of your team. I will happily move into the spare room at the station. I have, after all, stayed there, as you put it, 'in times past.'"

"Now you're being reasonable." Blair gave Silas a frosty smile. "I'll have to take a look at your place to make sure it's up to scratch, of course."

"It's most irregular," said Mr. Johnson, "but we will have a proper room available for Mr. Blair tomorrow. Perhaps it will be all right just for one night."

"It will be fine, Johnson," said the colonel, who, having used the entrance to his family's private wing and missed the preceding altercation, now appeared in the reception area. "As long as it's all right with you, Sergeant Macbeth."

"It will"—Hamish was breathing heavily to bring his temper, as famously fiery as his hair, under control—"be chust fine wi' me."

Silas took Blair off to inspect his room and the colonel pointed Hamish towards the bar.

"How about a wee dram?" he said. "That will help get rid of the taste of that terrible man."

"Thank you," said Hamish, calming himself. "It will take more than a dram, but that will be a start."

They walked into the bar, where the detectives were sitting around a corner table. One was carrying a tray of drinks to his colleagues, puffing out his cheeks, sticking his stomach out, and chanting, "Whit, no room? Whit, no room?" The others howled with laughter, then quieted down when they saw Hamish staring at them.

"You seem to have quite an effect on them." Bland was sitting on a barstool, swigging from a bottle of Coke.

"They're just letting off steam, Mr. Bland," said Hamish. "Unlike their boss, I'm sure they're decent lads."

"Put those on my tab, please," Bland said to

the barman when the drinks the colonel had ordered arrived.

"That's very kind of you," said the colonel.

"Not at all." Bland grinned. "I'm trying to make friends with the sergeant here, but he doesn't seem to trust me."

"You're right there," said Hamish, swallowing a mouthful of whisky. "It's hard to trust someone who doesn't tell you the truth."

"You got me." Bland raised his hands in mock surrender. "If I didn't tell you the exact truth, just let me know what you need me to clear up."

"You've been here longer than a couple of weeks."

"That's true, but it's a figure of speech. I said 'a couple of weeks' but I should have said 'a few weeks.' Six or seven weeks by now, I reckon."

"And the car is not rented."

"Again, that's not entirely untrue. I intended to rent it while I was here but then figured I might as well buy it. The value of most cars drops like a dead duck as soon as they leave the showroom, but cars like that Aston are different. Some of these babies go up in price real fast and you can make a bundle when you resell. It's what I do— buy low and sell high."

"And gamble." Hamish called for more drinks, offering one to the American, who preferred to stick with his Coke.

"Gotta keep a clear head for later tonight and tomorrow morning," he explained, smiling. "More buying and selling . . . and gambling. I play the stock markets, Sergeant—always a gamble. As soon as the after-hours session in New York ends, Shanghai and Tokyo are open for business. It pays to be a night owl."

"Hello, Hamish." Elspeth Grant walked into the bar. Her hair was sleek and straight, not the wild frizzy mane she had sported when working as a young reporter in the Highlands, and her tailored jacket and designer jeans were a far cry from the thrift-shop clothes she used to prefer. Her haunting silver-grey eyes, however, were the same—and as enticing—as ever.

"Elspeth," said Hamish, "I heard that you were—"

"Yes, hello, Hamish." Priscilla Halburton-Smythe strode into view from the other direction. She was taller than the slightly built Elspeth, and perfectly attired, as always, her dark blue cashmere jersey and skirt showing off her slim figure and highlighting the smooth bell of her blonde hair.

"Ah, Priscilla, I chust wouldn't have guessed that . . ."

"Aren't you going to introduce us to your friend?" asked Elspeth.

"Aye, of course, umm . . ."

"I'm Priscilla Halburton-Smythe," said Priscilla, cutting through Hamish's obvious discomfort to accept Bland's handshake. "I used to be engaged to Hamish."

"And I'm Elspeth Grant," said Elspeth, also shaking hands. "I was also engaged to Hamish."

"And now I am." Dorothy appeared from the reception area, her dark hair flowing in waves down to a low-cut, grey V-neck sweater worn over black velvet jeans. She joined the group, looking wary and defensive.

"Well, it's verra nice to . . . ahm . . . see all of yourselves together in the flesh . . . or in the room, I mean, and . . ." Hamish winced but stood tall, despite feeling as though a column of ants was marching up his back.

"Circle the wagons, buddy!" Bland grinned. "They've got you surrounded!"

Elspeth and Priscilla burst out laughing and Priscilla took Dorothy's hand.

"You have to forgive us," she said, gently, "but

we couldn't resist putting Hamish on the spot."
Dorothy smiled, and her shoulders, previously
high and tense, visibly relaxed.

"Absolutely." Elspeth put a sisterly arm around
Dorothy. "You don't get many chances to put
one over on Hamish Macbeth. We knew you'd
be coming in here, and this was too good
to miss!"

"Hamish," Priscilla said, suppressing another
burst of laughter, "your face is an absolute
picture!"

"Aye, well." Hamish sighed. "As long as you
had a good laugh..."

"Aww, come on, buddy." Bland planted a hand
on Hamish's shoulder, chuckling. "That was a
real good setup, admit it. They played you for
a patsy. Now lighten up and let me get us all
another drink."

The arrival of the three women had not gone
unnoticed at the detectives' table. The murmurs
of approval from the group turned to groans of
dismay when Blair appeared.

"Wheesht now and give's a drink," Blair
slurred, hushing the group of police officers in a
low voice. "I can tell you a thing or two about
those three beauties..."

The colonel tried to insist that the group now gathered around Hamish should join him and his wife for dinner as their guests but Elspeth had arranged to eat with her camera crew, Dorothy had decided on a light supper in her room, Bland needed to check on the markets, and, having drunk too much to drive, Hamish opted to walk home to feed Lugs and Sonsie. The dinner was postponed until the following evening. When the others had drifted off, Elspeth and Priscilla were left at the bar.

"Well," said Priscilla, "what did you think of her?"

"She seems perfectly respectable."

"Is that really what you think? You don't get a sense that there's something peculiar going on there?"

"You mean with the gift? I thought you didn't believe in that sort of thing."

"Well . . ." Priscilla swirled the ice in the remains of her gin and tonic. "We may not always have been the best of friends, but I think we know each other well enough nowadays to trust one another, and I trust your judgement, whether you're using your second sight or not."

"And we both have Hamish's best interests

at heart. I don't think marrying her will make him happy."

"You agree there's something weird about Dorothy?"

"Not just weird." Elspeth sighed, placing her empty glass on the bar. "Dangerous. She needs to look over her shoulder. There's a devil standing in her shadow."

CHAPTER FIVE

*The jealous are troublesome to others, but
a torment to themselves.*

William Penn

Dougie Tennant was exhausted. He wandered
into his cottage living room with Runrig blasting "Loch Lomond" in his earphones. Through
the darkness outside his front window he could
see the big police van parked on his starkly lit
filling station forecourt just two hundred yards
away. He shuddered. There were far fewer police
officers there now than there had been earlier,
but they were a constant reminder of what had
happened. He shook his head, as though that
would dispel the image of the bloodied car
interior and the horrific sight of the man's body

with that grotesque bullet hole in his temple. He sighed and turned towards the kitchen. Maybe a dram or two would help to settle him.

The solid steel spanner hit him full in the face, breaking his nose and sending him crashing to the floor. Dougie caught a fleeting glimpse of a man dressed in black and wearing a black balaclava that obscured all but his eyes. Then his hands flew to his head to try to fend off the fury of blows that rained down on him. He curled into a ball, scarcely able to draw breath, brutal kicks and bone-crunching blows from the spanner sending shockwaves of agony through his body. He felt himself begin to pass out, then the beating stopped and he recognised a familiar smell. Petrol. Unable to move, unable to scream, even through his closed eyelids he could see the sudden brightness of the flames.

Hamish Macbeth woke from a fitful sleep to the sound of his phone ringing at his bedside. He checked the time. It was four in the morning. He reached for the phone. It was Jimmy Anderson.

"Get yourself ower to Braikie hospital. It's Dougie Tennant. He's in intensive care."

"Dougie? How? What happened?"

"He was beaten half to death. I'm on my way there now."

Wrestling with his clothes, Hamish thundered down the stairs and was sprinting along the road in the direction of the hotel to pick up his car by the time a sleepy Silas appeared on the landing. Lugs sat on the threadbare rug, staring at him.

"What the hell's going on, Lugs?" Silas yawned, then caught the look of concern in the dog's eyes. "Whatever it is, we'd best be awake. Time for an early coffee."

Hamish pulled into the hospital car park in time to see Jimmy stepping out of his car. He caught up with him at the main entrance.

"I told you to make sure they looked after Dougie!" he roared.

"Remember who you're talking to, laddie!" Jimmy snapped. "I'm still your superior officer! I did make sure they looked after him. He answered what questions he could and he was escorted to his cottage, where he asked to be left alone."

"Did you not leave a guard with him?"

"They were guarding the crime scene. His cottage wasn't a crime scene."

"Well it is now! What happened?"

They were walking briskly along the bright hospital corridor, heading for the intensive care unit.

"One of the officers on duty is a smoker. He was warned not to smoke by the petrol station, but was gasping for a cigarette and took a wee walk along the road. He spotted flames in Dougie's cottage and ran down there. He found Dougie on the floor and got him out."

They were directed to the room where Dougie was with the medical team and met a doctor at the door.

"How is he, Doctor?" Hamish asked.

"Broken nose, fractured skull, fractured cheekbone, broken wrist and fingers—probably defensive wounds—broken ribs, severe bruising all over his body, smoke inhalation, concussion..." The doctor sighed. "Quite frankly, he's lucky to be alive."

"Is he going to make it?" asked Jimmy.

"He's in a really bad way, but his breathing is good and he has been stabilised for the time being."

"Can we see him?" Hamish moved towards the door but the doctor held out an arm to block his way.

"Only through there," he said, pointing to an observation window that looked into the room. "He's had painkillers and something to help him sleep. I don't want anyone near him except my staff."

Hamish and Jimmy stared in through the window. A nurse was fussing around Dougie's bed while another updated a chart. Dougie was hooked up to monitors that blinked green lights and an intravenous drip that hung from a stainless-steel stand. His face was so swollen and distorted that Hamish could barely recognise him.

"I did this," said Hamish, quietly. "I'm the one that persuaded him to get involved with the racers. That's what led to this."

"I bet he was glad to help." Jimmy watched the doctor hurrying off down the corridor. "Dougie's a decent lad. This is not your fault, Hamish."

"I'll wait here until he wakes up."

"No, Hamish." Jimmy pointed to two uniformed officers approaching. "I'm posting men here to guard Dougie. You need to get out and find who did this."

"I'll find him," Hamish vowed. "I'll find him, and he'll regret it."

* * *

"Breakfast?" Dick Fraser was standing beside Hamish's Land Rover holding an armful of large white paper bags from which steam rose gently into the cool, early morning air.

"You're a sight for sore eyes, Dick." Hamish smiled, crossing the hospital car park towards him. "How did you know I was here?"

"Silas called. He did some phoning around, found out where you'd gone in such a hurry and let me know that you'd probably need feeding. The bakery's just round the corner, after all. How's Dougie?"

"He took a real beating, but he's alive."

"That's something, at least. Poor Dougie. Never harmed a fly in his life. Take these. Silas said you wouldn't have time for anything if you had to collect Dorothy and then head straight out. I've done you a bacon bap, a sausage and bacon, and a bacon and egg."

"That's grand, Dick. I'll have them on the road back to Lochdubh."

"And there's a flask of coffee."

"Real coffee like you and Anka make? Fantastic, Dick!" Hamish rubbed the stubble on his chin. "Pity I'll not have time to tidy up afore we leave for Ardersier."

"Take this." Dick handed him a box. "It's an electric razor. New batteries. Never been used. I won it in a quiz."

"You're not still doing quizzes, are you, Dick? I thought you and Anka would be too busy now with the bakery."

"No more quizzes," Dick said, shaking his head, "but I need to get rid of a lot of the stuff that I won over the years, so you keep the razor."

"Thanks, Dick." Hamish climbed into the Land Rover. "I'll see you soon."

"You will." Dick grinned. "Saturday—at the wedding!"

"Culloden," Dorothy read from the signpost. "I always thought that the Battle of Culloden was down south, near Stirling."

Hamish glanced across at her, looking surprised, then fixed his eyes back on the road. There had been little said since they left Tommel Castle. Hamish was plagued by the vision of Dougie lying in the hospital bed, plugged in to monitors and drips. The notion that he was responsible had dragged him into a dark mood, and he was now driven by the thought of finding the man who had left Dougie helpless to die on the floor of his blazing cottage. If that was the same man who had shot Graham Leslie, so much the better, but finding Dougie's attacker was now the main focus of his attention.

Their route had taken them south, travelling the length of Loch Broom, then heading inland past Loch Droma, Loch Glascarnoch's dam, and the four-hundred-year-old Aultguish Inn before catching a glimpse of the giant wind turbines on the moorland skyline of Corrie-moillie Forest. The magnificent Kessock Bridge took them over the Beauly Firth north of the harbour at Inverness where the road skirted the city, declaring itself the "Highland Tourist Route to Aberdeen," before the signpost to Culloden had appeared.

"Bannockburn is near Stirling," he said.

"That's what I'm getting mixed up," Dorothy replied, searching for some way to feed the embers of conversation and distract him from dire thoughts about Dougie. "Culloden and Bannockburn. I never was much good at history."

"Bannockburn is a hundred and forty-five

miles south and was more than four hundred and
thirty years before Culloden. At Bannockburn,
Robert the Bruce won, and he made Scotland
an independent nation. At Culloden in 1746,
Bonnie Prince Charlie lost, and independence
was lost, too. You'd not mistake the two if you'd
ever stood on Culloden field. It's not a happy
place. Fifteen hundred Highlanders died there
in just one hour. Fort George was built to make
sure there was never another Highland uprising.
There's been soldiers there for over two hundred
and fifty years."

"Wow—more Wikipedia?"

"Some things stick in your mind. Highland
families have long memories. This is where we
turn off."

They swung left onto a road that took them
around the periphery of Inverness airport. With
the grey waters of the Moray Firth to their
left, they drove through the village of Ardersier,
taking the Old Military Road out onto the flat
spit where the fort hunkered down behind its
ramparts. This was not a showpiece castle of
the kind built by conceited aristocrats to flaunt
their wealth and status. In fact, far from providing a public display of extravagance, the grassy

ramparts, designed to absorb cannon fire, almost hid the fort from view. Fort George was a practical, functional, easily defended military base.

There was a tourist car park for those visiting the base and its regimental museum, but Hamish followed the road that clung to the coast, running between the massive stone defences and the sea, before turning into a tunnel that took them through the outer walls. An armed sentry wearing desert beige and sandy green camouflage—which Hamish couldn't help thinking wouldn't hide him very well on a lush Highland hillside—stopped them at the end of the tunnel, consulted a clipboard, and confirmed that they were expected. He directed them to a parking spot near one of the main blocks of solidly martial, red-stone, three-storey buildings.

"This is a huge space." Dorothy took in the views of enclosed parade grounds and quadrangles, and the expanses of outlying lawns clipped to military precision.

"Aye, it's a fair size, right enough," Hamish agreed, watching two soldiers hurrying past, their beige tam o' shanter bonnets, like that of the sentry, sporting the bright red hackle plume of the Black Watch. Hamish scratched his head and marvelled at the sense of urgency that pervaded the ancient fort. He knew that the base was not on any kind of alert and that the men and women were not preparing to be shipped off to some far-flung corner of the globe. There were few soldiers to be seen, yet there was still a sharp, expectant air, as though something big could happen at any moment. It was a far cry from the sleepy atmosphere he was used to in Lochdubh.

"Sergeant Macbeth?" A soldier stood in a doorway, beckoning to them. "This way, please."

They were led along a narrow corridor to an office that Hamish judged, from the outside, to be no bigger than a store cupboard. The door was open and an officer sat at his desk, flicking through some paperwork. He stood when he heard them approach.

"Come straight in." The officer stood to shake their hands, introducing himself as Captain Munro. "Please take a seat."

There were two plain wooden chairs in front of the captain's desk. On the desk was a neat pile of papers, a laptop computer, and a telephone. The only other furniture in the room was a filing cabinet. If not for the window that looked out onto a courtyard, Hamish would have revised his assessment from broom cupboard to punishment cell.

"Now," said Munro, settling into his seat, "what is it that you want to talk to young Bain about?"

Hamish estimated Munro to be in his early thirties. He was tall and his uniform hung from his slim frame as though it had been borrowed from a bigger man. His angular features gave him the look of a scholar, but his confident smile and restless dark eyes imparted an energy that left Hamish in no doubt that he was far more at home on a mountainside or an assault course than he was behind a desk. It was the same energy that pervaded the entire fort.

"We want to talk to him about his motorbike," Hamish said.

"I understand it was stolen." Munro glanced at his laptop screen and clicked a few keys. "Yes, in Dundee, when he was dealing with all the formalities of putting his mother's affairs in order following her funeral."

"What did she die of?" Hamish asked.

"That's the sort of thing that he can tell you himself, should he choose to."

"What's he like as a soldier?"

"One of my best. He's part of our new reconnaissance platoon. Excellent field skills. Excellent weapons skills. I wish I had more like him. But what does that have to do with a stolen motorbike?"

"We are investigating an incident that happened over near Scourie and we believe that whoever was riding Bain's bike might have information that could be useful."

"I see. Obviously I will encourage him to give you his full cooperation." Munro craned his neck towards the open door. "Mackay! Send in Lance Corporal Bain."

There came a quick-time stomp of marching boots and a soldier appeared in the room, stamping to attention near the desk. Neither he nor Munro were wearing their tam o' shanters, and no salutes were exchanged.

"At ease, Bain"—Munro was looking at his laptop again—"and stand easy. Close the door, would you? These police officers would like to talk to you about your motorbike. I will sit in on this conversation. Go ahead, Sergeant."

There was no seat for Bain. He stood by Munro's desk, shrinking the small room even further. He was neither as tall nor as slim as Munro, but he had an athletic build, blue eyes that glinted beneath a dark brow, and a shock of dark curly hair, shaved close at the sides and back.

"Where were you yesterday morning?" Hamish asked.

"On my way back by train from Broughty Ferry, just outside Dundee. My bike was stolen, so I had to get the train. Changed at Perth. One o' my mates picked me up from the station in Inverness."

"Do you have your tickets?" asked Dorothy. "Did you use a credit card?"

"Paid cash," Bain explained, "and ditched the tickets. We've not much room for clutter here."

"And where were you last night?" Hamish watched the young man's face for any tell-tale signs, any slight hesitation or even a sideways glance, that might indicate a lie.

"I went to Inverness with a couple of mates and had a few drinks."

"Is that allowed?" Hamish turned to Captain Munro.

"When we're in barracks, we work regular hours. Unless they have particular duties, our soldiers have most evenings and weekends to themselves. Generally we want them back here at a reasonable hour and in a reasonable state."

"Have you found my bike?" Bain asked. "When can I get it back?"

"We have found your bike," said Dorothy, "but you won't be getting it back any time soon. It's part of an enquiry into an incident near Scourie yesterday."

"Not that murder, was it?" Bain sounded animated. "I saw that on the news."

"Do you ever take the bike over that way?" Hamish asked.

"Not really." Bain shrugged. "Furthest west I go is usually Ardullie, just beyond the Cromarty Bridge."

"Why there? That can't be more than an hour or so round trip. That's not much on a powerful bike like yours."

"The Wee Kitchen. It's a burger van on the A9. Gordon's the chef and he does the best burgers anywhere. If I wanted a longer run, I'd take the bike down to Dundee, but that was before my mum . . ."

"We're sorry about your mum, Keith," said Dorothy. "That must have been tough for you."

"Aye, well, it's no secret that she was a druggie. She'd kicked the habit, though. She tried really hard and she got off the stuff, but the damage had been done over the years. She had a heart attack."

"Do you wear leathers when you're on your bike?" Hamish asked.

"Aye, I've a set o' black leathers."

"Can we take a look at them?"

Bain looked to Munro.

"Off you go and get them," Munro said. "Be quick about it."

Bain raced off down the corridor, and Munro addressed Hamish.

"You said nothing about murder. Do you believe Bain was involved?"

"That's what we're trying to find out," said Hamish.

Bain arrived back in the room, stamped to attention, and held out his motorcycle leathers, suspended on a clothes hanger. Hamish stood to take the hanger and examined the left side of the leathers. He showed Dorothy the scuffs, scrapes, and small tears running down the left leg and on the left hip. The rider they had been chasing had slid along the road on his left side.

"You've a bit of damage here," he said to Bain. "Come off your bike recently?"

"I've come off now and again," Bain admitted, turning the leathers over to show Hamish the other side. "This side's worse. These leathers have saved my hide a few times."

"We might want to talk with you again," Hamish said, handing the leathers back to Bain. "You're no going anywhere any time soon, are you?"

"There's the orienteering exercise . . . sir?" Bain again looked to Munro.

"Ah, yes," said Munro. "There's a team going out into the Cairngorms. Problem solving, map reading, finding their way from A to B, and so forth." He clicked a few more keys on his laptop, then looked up at Hamish. "I think I'll join them. It's about time I got out of this office for a while. We go out tomorrow and will be back late on Friday. Are you happy for Bain to be under my personal supervision, Sergeant?"

"That will be fine, sir." Hamish nodded.

A hint of drizzle whispered against the Land Rover windscreen, the sunshine that they had enjoyed for their trip to Fort George having been banished by a screen of light clouds. Hamish fastened his seat belt but paused before starting the engine.

"It was him," he said slowly.

"You mean Bain?" said Dorothy. "Bain killed Leslie and tried to kill Dougie?"

"That I can't yet say, but it was him that I chased up that hill. I could tell by the way he moved, by the way he held himself. It was him, all right. He was riding that bike."

"But he reported the bike stolen when he was in Dundee."

"That was him trying to create an alibi. He reported his bike stolen, but what if it wasn't? What if he rode it up to Sutherland and is lying about taking the train? That way, if the bike was spotted, he could claim someone else was riding it. But it wasn't someone else—it was him. He's lying. All we have to do is prove it."

"Maybe we should visit Inverness station. We can see if there's any CCTV of Bain leaving the station around the time the train came in from Dundee."

"That's a good place to start." He turned the key in the ignition, switched on the wipers, and headed for the tunnel that would take them out of Fort George.

"You seemed happy enough for Bain to go on the orienteering course," said Dorothy.

"Aye, and he's not likely to disappear with Munro keeping an eye on him. Besides, Blair and his boys will know about the motorbike by now, and if Bain's halfway up a mountain somewhere, they can't get their hands on him. That just might help to keep us one jump ahead."

"Whit was the point o' that? Have you gone completely bloody mental?" Not for the first time, Detective Chief Inspector Blair was struggling to keep his voice, and his temper, under control. "Well, it's not exactly made things easy for me, has it? Tell her I need to speak to her! I don't care—get her to phone me back!"

Blair let out a howl of rage and hurled his phone across the Tommel Castle car park where, like a pond skimmer thrown by a child, it skipped across the gravel, coming to rest against the tyre of James Bland's Aston Martin.

"You got lucky." Bland stooped to retrieve the phone, then held it out to Blair. "Looks like it's still working. What's up, buddy?"

"Mind your own bloody business, Yank!" Blair snarled, snatching the phone.

"You're welcome." Bland smiled. "Any time."

"You think you're pretty clever, don't you?" Blair's stubbly, booze-bloated jowls quivered. "Wi' your smarmy ways and your shiny car. Well, I've been watching you, and there's something fishy about you, pal. Whatever it is, I've no time for it now, but you'd better not cross me, Yank. I'm warning you . . ." His phone sprang to life in his hand, blasting out the theme tune to *Scooby-Doo*, a ringtone he had set by accident but could never figure out how to change.

"I guess that's Shaggy calling." Bland grinned.

"What is it?" Blair barked into his phone as he turned and stomped off in the direction of the hotel. "Oh, is he? I'll be right there." He scurried away to find one of his team to drive him to Braikie hospital, where Dougie Tennant had regained consciousness.

"I must apologise for his behaviour, Mr. Bland." The colonel joined Bland by his car, having witnessed the exchange from his patio. "But we're stuck with him. It seems he may be here for longer than we first thought."

"It's not a problem," said Bland, lowering himself into the car, "and please, call me James. Looking forward to seeing you at dinner tonight."

The colonel waved Bland off, looking down the rhododendron-lined driveway, listening to the throaty burble of the car's engine fade into the distance and thinking what a delight it was to have pleasant, well-mannered guests like Bland staying at his hotel. The sound of Blair grunting with the effort of jogging towards an unmarked police car and then whining at his driver reminded the colonel what a trial it was to have to put up with guests who were neither pleasant nor well-mannered. Not for the first time he considered erecting a sign on the driveway saying No RABBLE. No SCUM. No CRETINS. That, however, as he well knew—because Priscilla regularly reminded him—would not be good for business.

The images on the screen were far from perfect but Hamish was in no doubt when he spotted a man wearing a dark hoodie meeting another young man outside the station. When the man removed his hood, it was clearly Keith Bain.

"That's outside the station," Dorothy commented, sitting at a computer to search its files, "so we know Bain was telling the truth about one of his friends picking him up yesterday."

"Aye, but did he get off the train that came

north from Dundee and Perth?" said Hamish, crouching behind her. There wasn't much space in the windowless, dusty room into which the station manager had shown them, and there was only one chair at the desk. "We need to see the camera that shows the platform where that train came in."

"That should be here," said Dorothy, filling the computer screen with the image of a train pulling into the station. They watched a number of passengers stepping onto the platform, and a small crowd formed heading for the exit. "Could that be him there in the crowd?"

"That's him all right," Hamish agreed, "but we can't be sure that he actually got off the train. We can see him in that crowd, but there's not a good view of him leaving the train." He ran a hand through his hair, then added, "How about arrivals from Lairg earlier yesterday? There can't have been many."

Dorothy pulled up images of passengers on a different platform, exiting the Lairg train.

"There!" said Hamish, pointing at an elusive figure in a hoodie who disembarked and then disappeared into a shadowy area in the blink of an eye. "I'd swear that was Bain! He didn't come

in from the south, he came in from Lairg. I bet
he checked out the station days ago, figured out
where the cameras were, and worked out how to
avoid them. He hid somewhere in the station,
then mixed with the crowd, making it look like
he arrived on a completely different train."

"He's carrying a small rucksack. He could
have his bike leathers in there. Maybe he ditched
the helmet."

"You're right. It would be hard to hide a motorcycle helmet, and it would look too conspicuous
carrying it around. We should have asked to see
his helmet as well as his leathers."

"He seems to have planned this pretty well.
My guess is that he's got a spare. He could
get away with having a replacement helmet that
looked the same as his old one, but if he
suddenly had totally unmarked new leathers, his
mates would notice, so he kept the old ones."

"That makes sense. That video's not good
enough to be real proof that he came off the
Lairg train, but these cameras are a good line
to follow. There should be video we can check
to see if he got on the train in Broughty Ferry
like he said."

"If he lied about his bike being stolen and

lied about getting the train in order to cover up the fact that he was on his bike riding around Sutherland, then he must have had a very good reason. He needs an alibi and he needs to keep his presence in Sutherland a secret. That has to make him our prime suspect."

"But we need a motive. What connects him with Leslie? And could he have got back there last night and done that to Dougie?"

"That's what we have to find out."

"Aye, and we will." Thinking of Dougie reminded Hamish of the hospital. "Let's head home. We can call in at Braikie on the way."

Hospitals ranked pretty high on Hamish's list of least favourite places, somewhere up there with prisons and cemeteries. He liked the fact that hospitals were bright and clean, and he didn't mind the sharp smell of disinfectant, but there was no getting away from the fact that, like prisons and cemeteries, most people who were in hospital really didn't want to be there. Walking into Braikie's intensive care unit, it was easy to spot one of those people—the bored police constable standing guard outside Dougie's room.

"I'm not supposed to let anyone in, Sergeant,"

said the constable as Hamish and Dorothy approached.

"I'll not be long." Hamish opened the door. "He's a friend. I need to let him know I was here."

Leaving Dorothy chatting with the constable in the corridor, Hamish crossed the dimly lit room to Dougie's bedside. The monitors and the intravenous drip were as before, but the swelling around Dougie's face had now turned a deep purple and black, making him look even worse.

"Dougie," Hamish said in a soft voice, taking a seat by the bed. "It's me, Hamish."

Dougie's eyes flickered open and he made a croaking noise, trying to speak.

"No, Dougie, don't try to talk."

But Dougie reached for Hamish's hand and tried to draw him closer. Hamish leant forward, putting his ear close to the mouth of his injured friend. He heard just one word: "Balaclava."

"All right, Dougie, I get it. He was wearing a mask, so you didn't see his face. That's not why we came. We just wanted you to know that we're here for you and—"

"What do you think you're doing?" The voice was hushed, almost a whisper, but it was the angriest whisper Hamish had ever heard. He turned to see a nurse striding towards him, before she clamped a hand on his shoulder with a grip far stronger than he would have given her credit for and yanked him to his feet. Out in the corridor she closed the door and turned on Hamish.

"Hamish Macbeth! Are you completely stupid? That poor man is in no condition to answer your questions!"

"But I wasn't asking any questions, Moira," Hamish defended himself, recognising the nurse as the one who had tended to him when he had been treated in the hospital on several previous occasions. "He's my friend and I just wanted to see how he's doing."

"I see." The nurse calmed herself. "Well, he's showing some improvement, but it hasn't helped having your fat detective in here shouting at him. I mean, he's lucky to be alive. The last thing he needed was that horrible man yelling in his face."

"Blair..." Hamish clenched his fists by his sides and looked towards the constable guarding the door, who nodded confirmation. Hamish turned back to the nurse. "Thon detective, DCI

Blair, is best kept well away from Dougie. He will do nothing but upset him. Can you keep him out, Moira?"

"He might be able to bully your chum here," said Moira, jabbing a thumb towards the constable, "but he won't get past me again."

"I'll bet he won't." Hamish smiled. "Thanks, Moira."

"Don't your friends Dick and Anka have their bakery near here?" Dorothy was looking expectantly right and left as they left the hospital.

"They do." Hamish looked at her and grinned. "We should drop in on them. They make the best coffee anywhere and there's always something tasty on the go that they like me to try out for them."

"I wasn't suggesting that we scrounge a snack." Dorothy laughed, then a look of concern crossed her face. "It's just that this whole thing with Dougie is really getting to you. Maybe they could take your mind off it all for a moment."

"Aye, there's nothing like one of Anka's fancy pastries to take your mind off things!"

It was almost as though Dick had been expecting them. He made a huge fuss at meeting

Dorothy for the first time and then showed them upstairs to the apartment where he and Anka lived above the shop, leaving an assistant behind the counter. Within moments, a mouth-watering array of pastries, including an intricately plaited apple strudel, still warm from the oven, was laid out on the coffee table in front of them.

"I'd just made this fresh," Dick said, pouring coffee, "and the strudel is one of my favourites."

"This is a very nice flat," Dorothy said, scanning the room. "Nice high ceilings, and the décor is lovely. Is that down to you or Anka?"

"Actually," Dick said, serving slices of strudel, "we're that busy with the bakery nowadays, we got a decorator in to spruce the place up. The kitchen is our pride and joy, but I can't show you because Anka is in there working on something special—top secret!"

As though summoned by the mention of her name, Anka appeared. Hamish had always been baffled as to why the glamorous, long-legged, auburn-haired Polish beauty had decided to marry the drab, stout, grey-moustached Dick Fraser. Before the two had gotten together, Hamish had lusted after Anka, trying desperately to get her to agree to a dinner date. Dick didn't seem to have tried hard at all. The two had just clicked and were clearly gloriously happy together. That was a joy to see, and now that he had Dorothy, he knew exactly how they felt. He stood to greet Anka and introduce Dorothy.

"It's so nice to meet you at last." Anka sat next to Dorothy on the sofa, her eyes dancing with excitement. "Are you starting to feel like everything's going mad with the wedding only a few days away? What's your dress like? No, don't tell me, of course you can't talk about it with Hamish here."

"I love the dress." Dorothy beamed. "I'm picking it up from Strathbane on Friday, but to tell you the truth, we've not had too much time to worry about the wedding."

"Aye, the murder and that dreadful business with Dougie." Dick wiped pastry crumbs from his moustache. "How is he, Hamish, and are you any closer to finding who did this?"

Hamish gave Dick a quick briefing on the case, knowing that his old friend had always had a good brain for police work, if not the inclination or desire to actually pursue criminals. When he had worked with Hamish, he was more often found baking in the kitchen or snoozing in a deckchair in the front garden than he was ploughing through files and reports.

"From the way you describe it all," Dick said, leaning back in his armchair, "this sounds like a gangland killing. Your murderer is now probably sitting in a bar in Glasgow watching his handiwork being reported on TV. And it doesn't seem to me like you think this young soldier is a murderer."

"Everything we know points to him," said Dorothy.

"But we've no evidence yet that links him to Leslie or suggests a motive." Hamish took a sip of coffee. "And he has a good alibi for the attack on Dougie. More than that, he doesn't really *feel* like a callous assassin."

"Your gut feelings have served you well in the past, Hamish." Dick slid another slice of strudel onto Hamish's plate. "What about the American?"

"He seems okay, but there's something a bit odd about him," Hamish said. "I need to find out more about him."

"Put in a call to the police in Chicago," Dick suggested. "You've got relatives all over the world. Surely you must have a cousin or a nephew or a niece there?"

"Not that I can think of," Hamish admitted.

"But I do." Anka went to a sideboard and found an address book in a drawer. She made a note on a slip of paper and handed it to Hamish. "Victor Zukowski—son of my mother's cousin who emigrated to the United States. He's with the Chicago Police Department. He'll be happy to help."

"Thank you, Anka." Hamish rose to leave. "And thanks for the coffee and cakes. Every bit as good as everything else you two bake. But we need to get going. I want to take a look at Dougie's place before we head back to Lochdubh."

CHAPTER SIX

O 'tis a lovely thing for youth
To early walk in wisdom's way;
To fear a lie, to speak the truth,
That we may trust to all they say!
Isaac Watts, "Against Lying"

"The devastation here has transformed what was the scene of a gruesome murder into what now looks more like a battlefield. The cottage has been extensively damaged. The roof has collapsed, and from where we are standing—as close as the emergency services will allow—it looks like the inside has been gutted. Fire crews fought for hours to bring the blaze at the cottage under control, working in incredibly dangerous conditions to prevent the flames spreading to the filling station, where thousands of gallons of fuel are stored in underground tanks.

"The owner of the cottage and the filling station, thirty-four-year-old Douglas Tennant, remains in critical condition in Braikie hospital's intensive care unit, under police guard. The police do not appear to have any suspects for the murder at the filling station or the attempted murder of Mr. Tennant. A spokesperson said that their enquiries are at an early stage."

Hamish stepped out of the Land Rover just as Elspeth was finishing her report. She told her camera crew to take a break and walked over to greet Hamish and Dorothy.

"Care to make a statement, Sergeant Macbeth?" She smiled.

"This is no laughing matter, Elspeth." Hamish frowned. "Dougie's in a bad way."

"I know, and I'm sorry about your friend," she said. "This is a terrible business."

"It is that," Dorothy agreed. "The cottage is a real mess."

"You've been here before," Elspeth said to Dorothy.

"Yes, with Hamish. When we found the body in the car."

"That must be it." Elspeth appeared slightly distracted. "You have a strong connection to this place."

"Is that what your second sight is telling you?" Dorothy shrugged. "That's no great revelation, is it? Seems to me that anyone who has found a murder victim shot in the head will have a strong connection to a place."

"Andy's down there," Hamish said, having spotted another man examining the wrecked cottage, watched by the police constable guarding the crime scene. "I want to take a closer look at the cottage with him."

"How are the wedding plans working out?" Elspeth asked Dorothy as they watched Hamish walking towards the scorched ruin.

"Everything is working out just fine," Dorothy answered.

"Must be difficult with all of this going on."

"We're coping."

"That's good to hear. No fear of cold feet, then?"

"What do you mean?"

"It's just that, this period just before the wedding is a stressful time for any couple. People get upset, even start talking about calling the whole thing off."

"Well, I am *not* calling off my wedding." Dorothy turned to Elspeth, her jaw set tight and her eyes sharp with anger. "And no one can make me—certainly not a high-and-mighty TV glamour puss like you, nor a snooty little rich girl like your friend Priscilla. Unlike either of you, with your failed engagements, my wedding is going ahead—and no one's going to stop it!"

"Hey, cool down, Dorothy. I don't want to stop the wedding. I want everything to be perfect for you and Hamish."

"Good!" Dorothy snapped, turning away to join Hamish. "Keep it that way!"

Hamish was standing beside a wiry, blond-haired young man whose checked shirt and jeans were marked with black soot stains.

"How bad is it really, Andy?" he asked, turning over the charred wooden arm of a kitchen chair with the toe of his boot.

"What the fire didn't get, the water from the fire crews' hoses ruined." Andy sighed, pushing his hair back from his face, smudging his forehead with soot as he did so. "I've been trying to rescue as much of Dougie's stuff as I can, but there's no more than a few bits and pieces, really. Your lot"—he jerked a thumb towards the constable—"don't even want me touching that."

"I'll get them to turn a blind eye," Hamish promised, "but what about the cottage itself? Could you and your boys rescue it?"

"Of course we can, Hamish." The other man grinned. "We're not just builders, we're miracle workers! The walls look sound, and I can scrounge a lot of the materials from other jobs, but there will still be some costs . . ."

"Don't worry about the money, Andy. Dougie must have had some kind of insurance, but I doubt it will cover everything. We'll work something out."

"It's such a shame." Dorothy slipped her arm inside Hamish's. "It looked like such a sweet wee cottage."

"It was," Hamish agreed. "Dougie has lived here all his life, and he'll be back here again as soon as he's able. We'll make sure of that."

Hamish dropped Dorothy at Tommel Castle and was just about to leave the car park when his phone rang. It was Mary Blair.

"Mary," Hamish said. "Funny you should

phone. I've been meaning to give you a call. How are you?"

"I'm fine, Hamish—I'm more worried about you than I am myself. Something weird is going on."

"Let me guess: Your husband is up to something."

"Right first time. You'll have run into him up there in Lochdubh, I suppose?"

"I have. He's been making a nuisance of himself, but he seems to be getting on with the job. Do you think he's planning something?"

"He's been working hard since we moved south to Glasgow. He's forever on the phone. I never hear much of it, but he talks to some woman, or about some woman, like they work together, almost like she's his boss."

"Could be. They've more women at senior ranks now than ever before."

"But it doesn't sound like police business, Hamish."

"Maybe he's having an affair."

"Ha! That'll be the day. No other woman would want him—and I'd know if he was carrying on with someone else. No, it feels like something more serious than that. I got the feeling it had something to do with you."

"Maybe he wangled his way onto the murder team to give him a chance to come up here and make me look bad."

"No, Hamish. He didn't want to go to Lochdubh. He was talking to somebody about sticking to a plan. He seemed to think that him being in Lochdubh could ruin everything. I just wanted to call you to say, you know, watch your back."

Hamish thanked Mary for her concern and reassured her that he could handle whatever her husband was plotting, but as he tucked his phone back into his pocket, he felt a cold dread at the thought of exactly what that might be. He would have expected Blair to jump at the chance of coming to Lochdubh with a murder squad so that he could throw his weight around and try to make Hamish look like a fool. So why was he so reluctant to head north? What had he managed to get himself tangled up with in Glasgow? Was he working with Glasgow gangsters? Could he be involved in the murder of Graham Leslie? Could he have orchestrated that from a safe distance? Surely he couldn't have anything to do with the attack on Dougie? Hamish shook his head. With Blair, anything was possible.

When Hamish arrived home, a tall man in a grey suit was standing with his back to a large black saloon car parked outside the station house. In front of him, craning their necks to look him in the eye and clearly undaunted by his stature, were the diminutive Currie twins, sporting their trademark camel-hair coats but now with the unfamiliar addition of blue berets, each worn sloping to the right at precisely the same angle.

"You can't park here," Nessie barked at the man. "This area is reserved for emergency services."

"Emergency services." Jessie nodded.

"I'm sorry, ladies"—the tall man remained calm and polite—"but who are you?"

"We work very closely with the local police," Nessie informed him. "We are their eyes and ears."

"Eyes and ears," Jessie agreed.

"Well, police officers need to sniff out clues," said the man. "Maybe you could be their eyes and ears *and* noses . . ."

"I'll handle this, Stevie." Hamish recognised the man as a detective sergeant from Strathbane. "This man is a police officer," he explained to the twins. "He's here on important business."

"He hasn't shown us his ID badge."

"ID badge."

"You've been watching too many American cop shows," Hamish admonished them as they scrutinised the identification offered by the detective. "We call it a warrant card."

"I'm the same rank as young Hamish here," Stevie said with a smile, offering Nessie one of his official business cards, "but I have to wear a suit instead of a jumper."

"We should have warrant cards." Nessie sniffed, accepting the business card.

"Warrant cards," squawked her sister.

"Aye, well, you'd best talk to Constable McIver about that." Hamish decided that, having created these formidable vigilantes, Dorothy had best deal with them. "Now I'm wanted inside. I take it I have a visitor, Stevie?"

"Aye, DCI Anderson has just let himself into your kitchen."

The Currie twins marched off together to keep the peace elsewhere in Lochdubh and Hamish hurried indoors. Jimmy was sitting at the kitchen table, a bottle of the Balvenie malt whisky and two glasses in front of him.

"A special dram," he said, opening the bottle,

"to celebrate your engagement. Come in and sit down now—I thought you'd never get here. I hear that Dougie Tennant is out of the woods."

"Dougie's tougher than he looks." Hamish accepted a generous measure. "It will be a while before he's back at his pumps, though."

"Then let's drink to his health." Jimmy downed his whisky and poured himself a hefty refill.

"I see you've got Stevie driving you, so I'll not be able to arrest you for driving drunk," Hamish joked. "Blair never had a driver when he was in your job."

"Blair never wanted a driver because he never wanted anyone to know where he was or what he was getting up to." Jimmy drained his glass in one long swallow and reached for the bottle again. "He still doesn't."

"I hear that he's been acting a bit strange," Hamish said, sipping his drink and refusing a top-up. "I think he might be more involved with this case than we realise."

"What do you mean?"

"I think he's been making the wrong kind of friends down in Glasgow."

"The man is his own worst enemy." Jimmy sighed. "He's aye up to no good instead of just concentrating on his job, and, let's face it, the job is hard enough." He produced a beige folder from his briefcase and slid it across the table.

"Graham Leslie?" Hamish thumbed through the contents. "I've seen this already."

"I've dug up a bit more on his background. It might help. It also seems that he was involved in a nasty fight in a pool hall in Glasgow last year. Three ended up in hospital and one of them died. The pool hall is one of many businesses owned and run by the Macgregor family. The casualties were from a rival gang."

"It was the Macgregors that Murdo Macleod got involved with, wasn't it?"

"It was," Jimmy said, nodding, "but that was a long, long time ago, laddie. I noticed that you didn't say anything when Dorothy mentioned the Macgregors. Thought maybe you'd forgotten."

"You never forget things like that, but I'm not very proud of what happened. Murdo was a fine policeman when he was stationed up here. We were like family at one point, but something happened to him when he went south to Glasgow. Destroying files, taking bribes, planting evidence, all for the benefit of the Macgregor family. It was a sad day when we found out what he was doing, Jimmy." Hamish finished his drink and Jimmy poured them both another.

"You found him out, Hamish. You made sure I got all the credit, but it was you that suspected he was crooked and put the case together. I got a promotion out of that and you got what you've always wanted—to stay right here in your own wee police station in Lochdubh."

"And what did Murdo get? He's still in the jail."

"Not anymore." Jimmy let out a long breath. "He hanged himself in his cell a few weeks ago."

"Murdo's dead?"

"Aye . . . apparently he just couldn't take it anymore. I can't begin to imagine what he went through when he was locked up. The Macgregor family couldn't protect him when he was in the jail. Every jumped-up little would-be hard man on the inside wants to make a name for himself by having a go at an ex-cop."

"The Macgregor family couldn't protect Murdo, but Leslie wasn't locked up. Why couldn't they protect him?"

"Maybe they tried. He might not have made it easy for them to keep track of him. I'm told that Leslie disappeared off the radar completely for a few months until he popped up here in Lochdubh."

"I wish he'd popped up and got himself shot somewhere else."

"But it happened here, Hamish, and we need to deal with it. So—how did the interview at Fort George go?"

"Bain's alibi for the murder doesn't really hang together, and I'm convinced he was lying to us."

"You think he's our man?"

"I don't see him as a murderer, but I'm sure he's hiding something. My cousin Flora's husband, Jamie, is a police sergeant in Dundee. He might know a bit more about Bain."

"What about the American?"

"I need to make a phone call to Chicago now to check up on him. So far we've got nothing that connects him to the murder aside from the fact that I saw him and Leslie waving a lot of cash around in the Tommel Castle car park."

"Best get on with it then, laddie." Jimmy stretched a hand towards the bottle as though to take it with him, then paused and gave it an affectionate pat, like a favourite pet. "Keep that safe and we can have another couple of drams before your stag do."

Hamish looked at him blankly.

"Have they not spoken to you yet? Freddy and Silas have got it all sorted out, on Dorothy's orders. We'll be in the side bar at Tommel Castle on Friday evening. They've invited everyone. I'll come by and pick you up."

"Thanks." Hamish smiled uncertainly. "I'll look forward to that." In truth, he had too much on his mind even to think about a boozy lads' night out, but it seemed like everyone wanted to celebrate his wedding, and as Jimmy left, he felt a flutter of excitement in his chest. It really was happening. He was getting married to the most beautiful woman who had ever set foot in Lochdubh, and they would be walking up the aisle in just three days' time!

There was a clatter of paws and claws, and Lugs and Sonsie crashed in through the flap in the kitchen door.

"Where have you two been?" Hamish laughed, stooping to welcome them both. "Down at the beach again, judging by the seaweed in your coat, Lugs. You'll be wanting dinner before I phone anyone. I've a nice bit of coley here for you, Sonsie, and some of your favourite venison sausages, Lugs."

✻ ✻ ✻

Though the temperature had been mild when the sun shone, the optimistic warmth of a Highland spring day can easily turn to a frosty night, especially when there is no cloud cover and what little heat that gathered during the day absconds into the clear evening sky. Hamish lit a fire in the hearth, enjoying the sweet, earthy smell of the burning peat and the promise of a warm house when he got back from dinner at the hotel. He sighed at the thought of sitting down to dinner with the colonel, his wife, Priscilla, Elspeth, and Bland. It was not the assortment of dining companions he would have chosen, and the whole arrangement seemed too awkward and contrived. He didn't feel comfortable about it at all, but he was confident that Dorothy would make sure everything went smoothly. That's the sort of thing, he thought to himself, that I will have to get used to. Once we're married, we will be invited everywhere as a couple. The faces of the dinner guests drifted through his mind, and he focused on Bland. Mr. Bland, he told himself, is the job at hand. With Lugs and Sonsie curled up at his feet in front of the fire, he reached for the phone.

"Sergeant Macbeth!" Victor Zukowski sounded bright and cheerful. "Anka told me you would be phoning. How can I help?"

"I'm interested in an American who's staying at our local hotel. His name is James Bland and he lives somewhere called Glencoe in your neck of the woods."

"Sure, I know Glencoe. Let me check him out." There came the rapid clicking sound of fingers on computer keys. "Has he been a bad boy over there in Scotland?"

"Not as far as I know, but we have a situation here and I just need to know that he is who he says he is."

"Well, I got a James Bland registered at an address in Glencoe, but as far as we're concerned, he's clean. Let me talk with a buddy of mine on the Glencoe PSD. He might know a bit more."

"What's the PSD?"

"Public Safety Department. They're the local cops, but they're also paramedics and firefighters. Anything happens in Glencoe, they're in the middle of it."

"Sounds a bit like my job in Lochdubh."

"I bet it is. Give me a few minutes and I'll call you back."

Hamish thanked Zukowski, placed the phone on a side table, and slowly made to stand up, trying not to disturb his snoozing pets. Both immediately looked up at him with big eyes.

"There's no fooling you two, is there?" Hamish smiled at them. "But you can't come with me this time, and I need to look out my best suit."

The dog and the wild cat looked at each other, then back at Hamish.

"Aye, I know it's my only suit—but that makes it best, second best, and all the rest."

Hamish had changed into his suit trousers and a fresh shirt and was contemplating polishing his shoes when the phone rang. It was Zukowski.

"Thanks for calling back so quickly," said Hamish. "Was your friend able to help?"

"He sure was. He says Bland lives in a real nice house in Glencoe. He lives alone but has regular visitors from New York. Everyone says he's a pleasant guy but he travels a lot and doesn't get much involved with the local community. He lives a quiet life. The PSD have nothing on him, not even a parking fine or a speeding ticket."

"Do you know if he's into cars?"

"He's into them big time. Drives an English car—a classic Aston Martin. My buddy pulled him over once just to get a closer look at the car, and he was happy to chat about it."

"He's driving an Aston Martin here, too."

"Like I said," Zukowski said, laughing, "he loves his cars. Apparently he says the Aston makes him feel like James Bond instead of James Bland."

"He's used that line here, too."

"Then it's definitely the same guy."

"He doesn't seem to be short of money."

"Glencoe is an affluent area. There are a lot of very wealthy people who live there. Bland claims to have made his money on Wall Street."

By the time they had finished their call, Hamish was in no doubt that Bland was exactly who he said he was. That, however, did not leave him in the clear. If anything, the squeaky-clean report from Zukowski made Hamish even more suspicious of the American. He's an odd sort, Hamish mused. He doesn't seem the type to live "a quiet life." That really doesn't fit. Could his life in Glencoe be some sort of cover? Could he be involved with organised crime? Do the Macgregors have American connections? Could Bland be an assassin like his alter ego, James Bond?

Hamish picked up the folder on Graham Leslie, then cast it aside. He hadn't the time to go through it again now, but he did have to make one more phone call.

"Hamish! It's so good to hear from you!" The genuine delight in Flora's voice brought a smile to his face. "The wedding's coming up fast, isn't it? You must be getting really excited—maybe a wee bit nervous?"

"I've not really had time to think about being nervous . . ."

"Well, of course you haven't. There's far too much to think about before the big day. Like sending out the wedding invitations. I take it ours got lost in the post?"

"Ah . . . it's chust that . . . you see, I . . ."

"Och, don't be daft, Hamish Macbeth. I'm only pulling your leg. We know fine that you're keeping it small and local. Good for you both. Things go completely mental when the whole family gets together."

"Aye, they always do get a bit out of hand," Hamish agreed, remembering how the last big family celebration had progressed from a quiet lunch into a riotous ceilidh followed by a midnight hill-race challenge. He had won, naturally, and was thrown in the loch as his prize. "But I've not phoned about the wedding. I'm working on a murder case and I need to ask Jamie if he can get me CCTV footage from Broughty Ferry station."

"No, he can't . . ." said Flora. "Not unless you come down here and tell us all about this lovely lass you're marrying."

"I could come tomorrow."

"Good. Jamie has the day off, so you can look at your TV thingies and then we can all go out for a nice lunch at the Ship Inn."

Hamish spoke briefly with Jamie, who confirmed that viewing the station's CCTV records wouldn't be a problem, then he glanced at his watch, realised that he was running late, grabbed his jacket, and dashed outside to the Land Rover. He had intended to walk to the hotel, but he was now way behind schedule. At first, he resisted the temptation to break the speed limit on the quiet road through the village, but then he switched on the flashing blue lights and put his foot down. He caught a glimpse of himself in the mirror and shrugged. "Fair's fair," he told his reflection. "This isn't really an emergency, but there's not many perks to this job."

His long legs took the steps to the hotel entrance three at a time and he arrived in the main bar only slightly late, only slightly out of breath. Priscilla, elegantly attired and faultlessly coiffured as always, gave him a welcoming smile and straightened his collar.

"Tuck your shirt in, Hamish," she advised. "You need to smarten yourself up. Your fiancée is looking particularly gorgeous this evening."

Then he saw her. Dorothy stepped out of the small crowd that had surrounded her and lit up the gloom of the bar with a dazzling smile. The smile faltered for an instant when she saw Priscilla with her hand on Hamish's collar but was restored in the moment that it took her to cross the room. She was wearing a low-cut black dress that left her pale shoulders almost bare, save for where her waves of lustrous black hair fell. Her long legs were accentuated by high heels, making it easy for her to reach up and kiss Hamish as she slipped a proprietorial arm through his.

"You look lovely," Hamish said softly, squeezing her hand.

"Lovely?" Priscilla rolled her eyes in mock exasperation. "Hamish Macbeth, you've gone all soppy—but is that the best you can do? 'Lovely?' Your fiancée looks absolutely *amazing*."

"Thank you," Dorothy said, snuggling even closer into Hamish's side, "but I'll settle for 'lovely.'"

"And that pendant you're wearing is very special," Priscilla noted.

"It is, isn't it? It's one of a kind. I saw a woman trying it on in a Glasgow jeweller's a few months ago. She went off to think about it and I knew I just had to have it, so I bought it on the spot." Dorothy touched the pendant, and there came the unmistakeable flash of diamonds when it caught the light. "It's a Celtic knot—gold inset with diamonds."

"It's beautiful." Priscilla studied the pendant. The gleaming gold formed three leaf-shaped interlinked loops from one continuous band carrying an impressive array of diamonds. "It's a Christian thing, isn't it? A Trinity knot—Father, Son, and Holy Ghost sort of thing?"

"It's far older than Christianity," Elspeth said, joining them, and Hamish stepped aside, excusing himself by saying that he needed to talk to the colonel. "In pagan culture the three loops may have represented earth, sea, and sky. It may also represent three facets of woman as a goddess."

"That could be us," Priscilla joked. "Three women, three goddesses."

"The three facets," Elspeth said, raising an eyebrow to Priscilla, "are 'The Maiden'—a woman's innocence; 'The Mother'—a woman's fertility; and 'The Crone'—a woman's wisdom. Which one would you be?"

"Please, not the Crone!" Priscilla laughed. "I was thinking it might be us as 'The Three Fiancées.'"

"It might," Dorothy said with a smug smile, turning to join Hamish, "but currently only one of us actually qualifies."

"I thought I was doing quite well trying to jolly things along just then." Priscilla sighed as she and Elspeth watched Dorothy sidle up to Hamish and once more wind a possessive arm through his.

"It was a good try," said Elspeth, "but I get the feeling that we may never be able to reach her. She will never trust us. She has too many secrets to hide."

A paunchy, slouched figure in an ill-fitting suit trundled into the bar. DCI Blair was accompanied by one of his Glasgow detectives, and his eyes were fixed on Hamish.

"Macbeth!" he roared. "I want a word wi' you, Sergeant!"

The room fell silent. Hamish tensed. His hazel eyes narrowed and he slowly placed his whisky glass on the bar. Dorothy touched his hand.

"There are people watching, Hamish," she whispered. "Just do as he says."

"Out here," Blair snarled, heading for the reception area. "Get your lazy arse over here NOW!"

Hamish followed the two detectives out of the bar and paused near the reception desk, Silas having intercepted Blair.

"Mind your language in this hotel, Mr. Blair," he said, "and keep your voice down."

"And you keep your nose out, sonny," Blair barked. "This is police business, and you're no police!"

"It's all right, Silas," said Hamish. "I'll deal with him."

"No, Sergeant, I will deal wi' you!" Blair was clearly furious, but he had a strange look of satisfaction threatening to bring a smile to his lips. "What's this I'm hearing about you interviewing a suspect at Fort George?"

"That was to do with a speeding incident

involving a stolen motorbike." Hamish tried a half-truth to throw Blair off the scent.

"Bollocks it was!" Blair growled. "On the day of the murder you went chasing after a soldier just minutes away from where a man was shot in the heid. You let the killer slip through your fingers!"

"When we tried to nab him for speeding," Hamish said slowly, controlling his temper, "we knew nothing about any murder."

"So you went to all the trouble of travelling to Fort George—which is not only miles off your patch but is also a military base—to follow up a minor speeding case? Do you think I can't see what you're doing? You're carrying out your own investigation behind my back, aren't you? You're doing this to make me look bad. That's what you're up to, isn't it?"

"And what have you been up to? I hear you've been making a right nuisance of yourself at the hotel, bullying the staff."

"*Questioning* the staff! They're all suspects as far as I'm concerned. In fact, I'm told you had a run-in wi' Leslie outside in the car park. That makes you a suspect, too!"

"Don't be so bloody stupid!"

"Just remember who you're talking to, Sergeant! I am your superior officer!"

"All right—don't be so bloody stupid, *sir!*"

"Did you hear that, Matthews?" Blair turned to his sidekick. "Did you hear what he just said?"

Matthews glanced from Blair to Hamish and back to Blair, clearly reluctant to be dragged into what he knew was a feud with a history as deep as the loch outside.

"Sorry, sir," he apologised, pointing towards the cramped office behind the reception desk where a small television was showing a football match in progress. "Didn't hear a thing. I was watching the football."

"Get out of my sight, you useless eejit!" Blair roared at the detective, quivering with rage, before turning to Hamish. "You better watch yourself, Sergeant," he said, pointing a chubby finger at Hamish's chin. "If I find that you've interfered wi' a murder investigation, I'll get you suspended and you can kiss goodbye to your bonnie wee police station!"

Blair stomped out through the front door, rounding on Matthews, who was skulking on the stairs.

"I need to get out of here," Blair declared.

"Drive me down to the pub. And when we get there, it's your round."

"He's had his lot going door to door through Lochdubh," Silas told Hamish. "Anybody that's even a wee bit reluctant to talk is told they'll be dragged off to Strathbane for questioning. Nobody knows a thing about the murder, of course, and the village is in an uproar. He threatened to arrest the Currie twins when they told him they reported to Dorothy and would only talk to her. He's been just as bad here, yelling at the staff when they couldn't answer his questions about Leslie. The colonel's had enough. He's been on the phone to Superintendent Daviot."

"Aye, the colonel told me as much." Hamish sighed. "Why does Blair always have to be such a problem?"

"He hates you. He's jealous of you."

"Jealous?"

"He's the complete green-eyed monster. You have everything he could ever want. You're taller than him, younger than him, far better-looking than him, and women like you. You're good at your job. You're happy doing what you do. People respect you. He's just a fat, ugly old drunk."

"Why did this all have to happen now?"

Hamish sighed again. "The murder, Dougie, Blair winding everyone up, and all just a couple of days before Dorothy and me are to be wed."

"That," Silas said, clapping him on the shoulder with a grin, "is a real bright spot on the horizon for everybody, Hamish. The wedding—it will be a rare day. Now, away in and enjoy your dinner. Freddy's pulled out all the stops for you. He showed me the menu—Cullen skink, followed by wild venison haunch steak au poivre, with cranachan for dessert."

"Aye, that does sound good," Hamish agreed, and the rumble from his stomach banished all thoughts of Blair. "Dorothy will love Freddy's cranachan."

Not only Dorothy but everyone in the colonel's private dining room was full of praise for Freddy's culinary skills. Freddy served each course himself with the help of a hotel waitress, and his thin frame swelled with pride when he was given a standing ovation at the end of the meal. He made a brief yet gracious speech thanking those who had helped in the kitchen, and Hamish was pleased to see how relaxed Freddy was as the centre of attention. He had once told Hamish that he had always wanted to be an actor, and Hamish had readily agreed with Dorothy when she had suggested Freddy as his best man. Freddy was sure to give a great speech at the wedding.

Despite the profusion of wine and liqueurs on offer, Hamish drank mainly water, explaining that he had a painfully early start the following morning with a long drive ahead of him. For the same reason, he was first to leave, and Dorothy walked with him to the hotel steps.

"That was a lovely evening," she said, shivering slightly as they hit the cool night air.

"You charmed them all, as usual," Hamish said, smiling, "but you should go back in. You're cold."

"How can I be cold with my big Highlander to keep me cosy?" Standing on the step above him, she slipped her arms inside his jacket and hugged him tight. "The colonel's wife seemed to be very taken with Mr. Bland. She was chatting to him all night."

"She'll be seeing him as a potential son-in-law."

"Like she once did with you?"

"Not quite the same. I wasn't from the right background to get the full seal of approval."

"Was that why it didn't work out between you and Priscilla?"

"No . . . we chust weren't right together."

"Well, we are right together." In her heels and standing one step higher, she had no need to raise herself on tiptoes to kiss him.

"I'm going to miss you tomorrow," he admitted.

"Someone has to be on duty here while you go gallivanting off to Dundee. Here—take these." She pressed her car keys into his hand. "Use my car."

"The Land Rover will do fine for me . . ."

"No, I will need the Land Rover here. I can't take my car out on calls, and you won't be in uniform—officially you'll be off duty. We don't want Blair finding out what you're doing, and you can keep a low profile if you don't turn up in a police Land Rover. Besides, my car will get you back here to me again far quicker!"

She hugged him close once more and kissed him again.

"After Saturday," she said, smoothing a lock of red hair from his forehead, "no more good-nights."

"That thought," he said with a laugh, retreating down the steps, "will keep me warm all the way home!"

She waved him off as he drove out of the

car park. Hamish had never actually paid any attention to Dorothy's car before, but he had to admit to himself as he motored through the village that her Mercedes saloon was a different beast to his old Land Rover when it came to comfort and refinement. *I wouldn't much fancy driving it across a peat bog,* he thought to himself, *but it will make the long trip tomorrow far easier.*

Screaming and swearing? Freddy's eyes popped open. He had heard many things blasting out from his radio alarm clock at dawn, but never a full-blown argument in the most colourful language. It took him only an instant to realise that the row was coming not from his radio but from downstairs—Dorothy's room! He leapt out of bed, pulled on a pair of jeans and a T-shirt, and dashed for the stairs, pushing buttons on his mobile phone.

"Silas—it's Dorothy!" He didn't wait for a response. He arrived outside Dorothy's open door to see her slumped on the floor at the foot of her bed, wrapped in a dressing gown and sobbing hysterically. He caught a glimpse of a woman hurrying down the main stairs.

"Dorothy!" Freddy rushed into the room and crouched beside her. "Are you hurt?"

"No, I'm okay," she whispered, sniffing and wiping her eyes with a tissue.

"What's happened?"

He put an arm around her and helped her into an armchair. Silas hurtled in through the door, hair tousled, barefoot and barely dressed.

"A woman," Freddy said, gesturing towards the corridor. "On the stairs."

Silas headed for the main staircase.

"Freddy, you mustn't tell Hamish." Dorothy was breathing deeply to banish the sobs. "Promise me you won't tell him."

"I won't," Freddy lied, "but what's going on?"

Silas arrived back in the room.

"She's gone," he panted, bending to recover his breath. "Had a car waiting. Who was she?"

"My oldest friend—at least I had hoped she was still my friend. It would seem not."

"It's four in the morning," Silas said, checking his watch. "The hotel was locked up. How did she get in?"

"I let her in," Dorothy confessed, looking up at them both, her blue eyes tinged with pink from crying and her cheeks wet with tears.

"A visitor at this hour?" Silas was perplexed. "Why in the middle of the night?"

"I begged her to come. She's catching an early holiday flight out of Inverness. I was trying to persuade her not to go. I wanted her to be my maid of honour at the wedding on Saturday."

"So how did that turn into a shouting match?" asked Freddy. "Did you fall out so badly over the wedding?"

"We fell out ages ago," Dorothy admitted, "over a man. I wanted to try to patch things up. Seems like I only made things worse. You won't tell Hamish, will you, Silas? You must both promise not to say anything. I don't want anything to spoil the wedding for him."

"I, well . . . no, of course not." The lie did not come as easily to Silas as it had to Freddy. "We promise, don't we, Freddy?"

"Aye, if that's what you want."

"It is. Thank you both. I think I'd like to try to get some sleep now."

Silas closed the door softly and the two former policemen walked quietly down the corridor together.

"I'm not sure she was telling us the whole truth," Silas said quietly.

"Not a bit of it," Freddy agreed, "but it was a fine performance. If she was an actress, she would have won an Oscar—real tears—the works."

"Do you think that was the same woman who asked about her before?"

"I reckon so."

"What were they really arguing about?"

"No idea. I heard the shrieking and bawling but I couldn't make out exactly what they were yelling. Why would anyone pick a fight with Dorothy in the middle of the night?"

"This is all really weird. We need to tell him."

"You promised you wouldn't."

"So did you."

"Aye, and I doubt she believed a word. We're far worse liars than she is."

CHAPTER SEVEN

My heart's in the Highlands, my heart is not here,
My heart's in the Highlands, a-chasing the deer;
A-chasing the wild deer, and following the roe,
My heart's in the Highlands, wherever I go.
Robert Burns, "My Heart's in the
Highlands"

Hamish was trapped. There was a crushing pressure on his chest pinning him flat on his back. He couldn't move his arms. He couldn't move his legs. With a surge of panic, he realised that he could barely breathe. He held his breath in horror, worrying that if he breathed out, the force pressing down on his chest would prevent him from filling his lungs with air again. He would suffocate, breath and life squeezed from his body. He wanted to scream but no sound came from his lips. He thrashed his head from side to side in terror. He was almost overwhelmed by the fetid stench of rotting garbage. Was this how it was to end? Was he to die crushed to a pulp in the back of a bin lorry? Then came the low throb of the compactor's engine, which sounded . . . familiar, not like machinery at all, more like . . . snoring. He woke with a gasp to find Sonsie asleep on his chest and Lugs draped across his legs.

"Get off the bed, you two!" he moaned, freeing his arms from beneath the duvet to push the big wild cat aside. "Sonsie, you stink worse than a binman's breeks! Have you been rooting around in somebody's rubbish?"

The wild cat gave him a look of mortified innocence, then stalked out of the room. If he didn't appreciate the aroma with which she had coated herself, she would take her charms elsewhere. Lugs bounced down from the bed and stood staring straight into Hamish's face. The dog's tail wagged madly and his odd eyes were shining with excitement. Not for the first time Hamish marvelled at how Lugs could go from sound asleep to wide awake in less than a heartbeat.

"Aye, well I suppose you'll both be wanting an early breakfast this morning." Hamish reached for his wristwatch on the bedside cabinet. It was not yet five o'clock. He looked out through the open curtains at the watery, grey, pre-dawn light, heaved himself out of bed, and headed down to the kitchen to feed his pets and make his first coffee of the day.

"So you're not rushing off back down to Glasgow, to defend your interests among the cut and thrust and deadly intrigue of the TV newsroom?" Priscilla lowered her china coffee cup onto its saucer and smiled mischievously across the table. Elspeth sat opposite, framed by the doorway to the Tommel Castle dining room.

"Not just yet." Elspeth's expression was far more sombre. "I'm due some time off, so I thought I'd stick around, stay for the wedding."

"And that handsome cameraman of yours—the one with the beard—is he sticking around, too?"

"We're just friends, Priscilla," Elspeth rebuked her breakfast companion, leaving her in no doubt how irksome she found the comment. "More importantly, did you hear the row that broke out last night?"

"Here in the hotel? No, I didn't hear a thing. The private quarters are pretty well insulated from the rest of the place. What happened?"

"Dorothy had a visitor in the middle of the night and it turned into a real catfight. Dorothy was in floods of tears and the woman ran off."

"A woman? Same one who was asking about her before?"

"I never saw that woman."

"Freddy said she was small, blonde, and middle-aged but younger looking."

"That could easily be a description of the woman I saw last night. Freddy and Silas would know if it's the same woman. They both saw her."

"Then we must question them," Priscilla decided, and, looking over Elspeth's shoulder, she held up a discreet warning finger. "Shush now. Here comes Dorothy."

"Come and join us, Dorothy," Elspeth said, turning in her seat and waving. Dorothy looked uncertain, hesitating for a moment before crossing the room towards them. She was in uniform, and she hung her hat and service belt over the back of her chair.

"A late start for you, isn't it?" Priscilla noted.

"It's almost seven-thirty. You're usually at the station by now."

"I just need a quick cup of coffee. I had a bit of a disturbed night," Dorothy admitted, stifling a yawn.

"So I heard," Elspeth said. "My room's just along the corridor from yours."

"Oh, no . . ." Dorothy buried her face in her hands. Her shoulders shook with silent sobs. "Not you, too."

"Ah, yes," said Priscilla. "The boys were on hand to help out, weren't they?"

"Freddy and Silas were great." Dorothy sat up, dabbing her eyes with a napkin.

"Chin up," Elspeth said softly, laying a comforting hand on Dorothy's shoulder. "We can't have a cop crying in public."

"So what was it all about?" Priscilla asked.

"An old friend—a former friend," Dorothy sniffed. "I had hoped we could let bygones be bygones and that she would be my matron of honour—the only guest at the wedding from my side."

"I take it she wasn't too keen." Priscilla poured Dorothy a coffee.

"We argued. Same old stuff all over again,"

Dorothy said quietly. "Now I will definitely have no one at the wedding."

"Nonsense," Elspeth gently chided. "Everyone at the church on Saturday will be there for you, not just for Hamish. We'll all be there for you. If you would like, Priscilla and I can be your bridesmaids, or joint matrons, or whatever. We'll be your supporters and go with you to the church, won't we, Priscilla?"

"Well, yes, of course . . ."

"Oh, that would be amazing!" Dorothy flung her arms around Elspeth, who gave her a hug. "Thank you both so much! This means the world to me." Dorothy then hugged Priscilla, who stiffened slightly but managed an almost affectionate pat on the back in return. "But we don't have to tell Hamish about last night, do we?"

"Not if you don't want us to." Elspeth squeezed Dorothy's hand. "Now tell us all about your plans for Saturday."

Dorothy chatted excitedly about her big day, finished her coffee, and then, bubbling with gratitude, strapped on her service belt and headed off to work.

"It was rather presumptuous of you to offer

my services." Priscilla's voice was quiet but cool enough to bring a chill to the atmosphere.

"I didn't think you would want to miss out on anything," Elspeth defended herself. "Besides, Dorothy is a real enigma. I get the feeling that anything could happen with her around."

"You think she might do something silly?"

"No, it's just that ... well ... things around here feel very strange at the moment."

"You don't need second sight to tell that things are a bit strange—murder, attempted murder, arson, and a mysterious woman popping in and out of the hotel at all hours of the night."

"Yes, but don't you see? Dorothy is mixed up in it all—I'm certain of that. I'm not sure that I can cope with her on my own."

"You won't have to." Priscilla sighed. "I'll be here, and then, in a couple of days, Hamish is the one who will have to deal with her."

"That's what worries me most. I really don't think he knows what he's letting himself in for."

"Not if that little episode is anything to go by." Priscilla examined Dorothy's napkin. "She faked the crying. No floods of tears this morning. Maybe she didn't want to spoil her make-up entirely. There's a bit of mascara on here but no tear stains. She was patting away at dry eyes."

"Are we maybe just being horrible and cynical and suspicious?"

"Yes, but not without good reason. Let's have a word with Freddy and Silas before we say anything to Hamish."

Hamish had paused for a moment on the bridge over the River Anstey as he left Lochdubh, looking down at the clear water swollen with melted winter snow, reeling in pools and swirling white skirts over rocks in a frantic dance towards the loch. The village was barely awake. He could see lights in Mr. Patel's store and an occasional glow from behind curtained cottage windows, early risers setting their morning in motion. The sky was a good deal lighter now than when he had first woken but the sun had yet to cast its full glory over Lochdubh. The white cottages lay half asleep, scattered along the edge of the loch, serenely unaware of whatever the day held in store for them. It was a beautiful setting, and every time Hamish had cause to leave, he felt like he was leaving part of himself behind. He worried what might happen to the town while he was gone. He told himself not to be so silly. It was foolishly vain to believe that Lochdubh needed him to take care of it. It could survive without him for a few hours, and the great consolation for the melancholy of his departure was the anticipated joy of his return.

That had been more than two hours ago, and now, having stopped for fuel and to stretch his legs at Aviemore, he was motoring down the A9, through the western reaches of the Cairngorm Mountains with the spring sun low in the sky. Squinting against the bright light, he scrabbled in the door pocket where he was sure he had seen one of Dorothy's many pairs of sunglasses, hoping not to bend them out of shape too badly when he squeezed them on. The road swung down into Glen Garry, following the river of the same name to Blair Atholl, ancestral home of the Duke of Atholl, Chieftain of Clan Murray and the only man in Britain to retain his own private army. Hamish had encountered the kilted warriors, the Atholl Highlanders, at Highland gatherings and judged them an impressive bunch, although perhaps better suited to ceremonial duties than the sort of work undertaken by the Black Watch.

That thought steered Hamish's mind back to Keith Bain. He was out there somewhere up in the mountains right now, probably dodging other squaddies on their training exercise just as he had hoodwinked Hamish on the hillside the day of the murder. Hamish was in no doubt that it had been Bain riding the motorbike, but how had he got himself involved in the murder? Could he really have shot Graham Leslie in the head? If he wasn't the murderer, why had he gone to all the trouble of creating an elaborate alibi? Maybe that alibi would fall apart completely when he viewed the CCTV footage. Hamish pressed on, bypassing Pitlochry and Dunkeld, before following the River Tay from Perth east towards Dundee.

In the twenty miles between Perth and Dundee the river became tidal and broadened from a few hundred yards to around three miles wide before narrowing again to half that distance where the Tay's rail and road bridges linked Dundee on the north bank to Fife on the south. Hamish followed the road past the airport into the centre of the city and continued east towards Broughty Ferry.

Beyond Dundee city centre, the skyline was

dominated by a brace of enormous oilrigs under-
going maintenance at the docks, and the traffic
began to ease. Although by no means a complete
stranger to big cities, Hamish found Dundee far
busier than Strathbane. The buildings seemed to
stretch for miles, yet he knew the city was still
ten times smaller than Glasgow. Approaching
the Broughty Ferry suburb, the character of the
city began to change slightly, becoming less of
a business and commercial centre and more of
a coastal town, in keeping with its history as a
fishing and whaling port.

Broughty Ferry police station was easy enough
to find. The wrought-iron Victorian lamp outside
with its blue-and-white chequered glass would
have been enough of a clue on its own, but standing beneath it, forewarned of his arrival by a phone
call from Hamish, cousin Flora and her husband
were waving enthusiastically. She was just as
Hamish remembered her. Although now a grown
woman, she still had the cheeky smile and mass
of blonde curls of the pretty girl he recalled from
years before. Her husband, Jamie—not quite as
tall as Hamish but with a broader build, dark hair
and eyes buried beneath heavy brows—directed
him towards the kerb-side parking spaces reserved

for police vehicles. While Flora delivered squeals and hugs, Jamie slipped a visitor's parking permit onto the car's dashboard.

"The traffic wardens around here can be a wee bit keen," he explained.

"We've no need of them in Lochdubh." Hamish smiled. "Even if we had the traffic, we have the Currie twins."

"I remember them!" Flora laughed. "Two lovely little old ladies, with one who always repeated the last thing said by the other."

"By the other," Hamish nodded, chuckling. "Stalwarts of the community. Lochdubh wouldn't be the same without them. How are your boys?"

"Growing fast and both at school," Flora said. "We won't see them again today until four o'clock."

"What do you think of our cop shop, Hamish?" Jamie presented the police station with a wave of his arm. It was built of local sandstone with large windows and a slate roof. Hamish estimated it was just a little larger than his own station, but, unlike Lochdubh police station, it had no garden separating it from the street.

"It's a bonnie building," Hamish conceded. "Not so different from mine, but I don't have one of those next door." He nodded towards the huge Marks & Spencer Food Hall to the right. "And Lochdubh is never as busy as this, even at the height of the tourist season."

"Speaking of busy," said Jamie, "we need to get along to the railway station. The manager promised a cup of coffee while we were looking at the CCTV stuff. He's a good lad and he'll have it all ready for us."

Flora opted to do some shopping and promised to meet them at the Ship Inn for lunch. Hamish and Jamie made their way along the street past a treasure trove of shops all bustling with customers. The river was now to be glimpsed only fleetingly between the buildings, but on the higher ground to the north Hamish could see the chimneys and gables of large stone villas. Built in the nineteenth century by Dundee jute barons to escape the dirt and grime of their mills, they turned Broughty Ferry into one of Europe's richest suburbs. It was a distinction that had faded with the dwindling of Dundee's industry.

The railway station sat by a level crossing, where traffic lights and red-and-white painted barriers controlled vehicles using the road that crossed the tracks. Hamish noted that there were cameras

covering the crossing as well as the station plat-
forms. If Bain had boarded a train here, they would
surely have him on film. Ushering them to a small
room upstairs and apologising profusely for not
being able to provide more comfortable facilities,
the station manager settled them at a computer
terminal, then bustled off to make coffee.

"These are the files from the day you asked
about," Jamie said, opening a folder on the screen.

"Let's check every departure. Looks like there's
more than a dozen, but if we've got him boarding
any of them, I'll recognise him. I know the way
that laddie moves."

"Aye, he's a proper athlete is our Mr. Bain."

"You know him?"

"I do. I first came across him not long after we
moved here. He got himself into a bit of trouble
when he was still living here with his mother.
All he ever wanted to do was to be a soldier. He
joined the Black Watch cadets down at Broughty
Castle while he was still at school and I used to
see him running along the beach in full kit, on
his own, training hard."

"What sort of trouble did he get into?"

"Well, I guess you know that Carla, his mother,
was a junkie for years. I'm told his father was a

dealer but he vanished when Carla got pregnant. She was clean for the last few years but never in good health. Young Keith saw first-hand the damage that drugs do. He hated everything to do with drugs.

"Just before his sixteenth birthday, he came across three lads hanging around his school, trying to tempt kids with pills and suchlike. He laid into them. Gave them a real beating."

"What did you charge him with?"

"Nothing. The only witnesses wouldn't give statements and none of the dealers wanted to press charges. They were small fry in the drugs business but they were hell bent on getting their own back."

"Folk like that take their vendettas seriously."

"That's what I thought, too. There were a couple of incidents. He told me he was threatened and that a local lout told him someone was coming to take care of him and his mother, then it all went quiet. Rumour was that the locals were ordered to lay off him. Word went round that he and Carla were to be left alone and that anyone who laid a finger on them would be kneecapped and chucked off the Tay Bridge. Those were just rumours, mind."

"It's a wicked world down here in Dundee." Hamish was studying the footage for any trace of Bain.

"Not so bad, really." Jamie smiled. "Not compared with where I used to work in Glasgow."

After an hour poring over the video footage, they had covered every train leaving the station on the day of Graham Leslie's murder and there was no sign of Keith Bain.

"I suppose he could have gone into Dundee to catch the train," reasoned Jamie.

"But he told us that he caught the train here. He didn't—that was a pack of lies, just like the rest of his alibi."

"Well, there's no more we can do here. Let's take a stroll before we meet Flora."

From the station, they walked down the street towards the river where, leaving the shelter of the buildings behind, the vista opened out on a vast expanse of water. The light was so clear and bright that the forest and sand dunes on the other side of the estuary, which Hamish knew must be a couple of miles away, looked almost close enough to touch. They strolled to the sandy beach dominated by Broughty Castle, the stone fortress that had stood guard over the mouth of the Tay for more than five hundred years.

"It's a fine view here, Hamish, eh?" Jamie grinned, breathing in great lungfuls of fresh air on a breeze that had sailed straight across the North Sea from northern Denmark. "Different from where you live."

"Different it is." Hamish gazed out across the water. "A lovely view but very different from Lochdubh." From the low hills across the estuary in Fife, he scanned up the river to the bridges and began to realise why this part of the country was so different from home. In Lochdubh they were surrounded by mountains that closed around the village like giants drawn by the scent and warmth of the peat fires, casting dark shadows over the loch. Here the low hills lay back from the water, giving the city room to spread and allowing the sun to play on the river, flooding the countryside with sharp light. This was a lovely setting, but Hamish thought of old McTaggart on his croft near Kylestrome when he admitted to himself, "This is Scotland, but it's not *my* Scotland."

The Ship Inn was a short walk along the waterfront from the beach, and they met Flora outside, who was beaming just as happily as she had when she first set eyes on Hamish. She had bagged a table in the bar by the window, looking out over the rescue lifeboat lazily stretching its mooring lines at the quayside. They each ordered haddock and chips and Hamish refused a beer, knowing that the journey home would take him at least the five hours he had spent on the road that morning. He answered a barrage of questions from Flora about the people and places she had grown up with in the Western Highlands. Jamie listened politely and joined in occasionally. He did not share all of his wife's memories, having been brought up near Glasgow, although the couple had lived in Dundee for more than five years. Their meal finished and plates cleared, they sat with cups of coffee until Flora could contain herself no longer.

"Come on now, Hamish," she said, laughing. "I've been waiting for you to mention this new lass of yours and you've said nothing. So now tell me—who is she, how did you meet her? And, most important, show me a photograph!"

"She's a police officer." Hamish smiled proudly. "She is the most beautiful girl in the world, but she doesn't much like having her photograph taken. I got this one when she wasn't looking."

He held up his mobile phone to show them the picture. "Her name is Dorothy . . ."

"McIver!" Jamie spluttered, spilling his coffee.

"Are you all right?" Flora frowned at her husband.

"Aye, aye, I'm fine." Jamie wiped his mouth with a napkin. "Just taken a bit by surprise, that's all."

"Why surprised?" Hamish asked. "Do you know Dorothy?"

"Not very well," Jamie explained awkwardly. "I used to know her a bit. We were in the same division when Flora and I were still in Glasgow."

"You were friends then?"

"No, no, not really. I . . . um . . . didn't much care for the company she kept."

"What are you talking about? What are you not telling me, Jamie?" Hamish was suddenly deeply suspicious of Jamie's reaction and wary of what he might hear next.

"Nothing, honestly. I just . . . wouldn't have thought that she was your type."

"What's that supposed to mean?" There was a hint of anger in Hamish's voice.

"Just that, when I knew her, she used to mix with a dodgy kind of crowd, hanging out in cocktail bars and nightclubs with some really sleazy characters—villains that most of us would rather see locked up than be seen drinking with."

"Sometimes we all have to do that," Hamish said, defending his fiancée. "Sometimes it's part of the job."

"I understand that, but it can be a risky game to play. These folk—if they think they've got their clutches into you, they never let go. Corruption, bribery, intimidation—they would stop at nothing if they thought it was good for business. They were ruthless, heartless, utter bastards."

"Why would that sort of thing involve Dorothy?" Hamish demanded. "And why am I now thinking that you're speaking from first-hand experience?"

"It's why we left Glasgow, Hamish," Flora chimed in. "Jamie was being threatened. Gangsters wanted him to do them a few favours, take a bit of cash for his trouble. If he refused, something bad would happen to me and the boys."

"Are you suggesting Dorothy played a part in that?"

"I'm not suggesting anything." Jamie held up his hands defensively. "We came here to get away from that stuff."

"And that's exactly why Dorothy wanted to come to Lochdubh."

"I hope so, Hamish. I hope she's left it all behind."

"Of course she has!" Hamish snapped. "She would never have been tangled up with the kind of scum you're talking about! She is the most loving and honest woman I have ever met, and she is to be married to me the day after tomorrow!"

"Calm down now, Hamish, please," Flora pleaded. "If she's won your trust, then she must be a good person and the bad old days in Glasgow are in the past. What's passed is best left in the past."

"I think I'd better go now." Hamish stood up to leave.

"Don't leave on a bad feeling, Hamish," Flora implored him, the joy that had lit up her face earlier now banished by the tears welling in her eyes.

"There's no bad feeling, Flora." Hamish sighed and let the tension in his shoulders subside. He stooped to kiss her on the cheek. "It's a long drive I have in front of me, and I need to get on the road. You're right—we should leave the past where it belongs. One question . . ." He turned to Jamie. "The Macgregors—were they part of it?"

"They were the worst of the lot."

Hamish lost no time in leaving Broughty Ferry behind him, but, having retraced his route beyond the centre of Dundee, his mind was spinning through the events of the day faster and faster, making it difficult to concentrate on the road. He pulled into a parking spot by the seawall near the Tay Rail Bridge and got out of the car. He needed to get his head straight. How could Jamie have thought that Dorothy could ever have been involved with the seedy Glasgow underworld? He knew that Jamie and Flora had left Glasgow in a hurry. He also knew that Jamie had been denied promotion more than once, despite having passed his exams to become an inspector, so he had carved out a nice little niche for himself in Broughty Ferry. Well, he couldn't be blamed for that—had Hamish not been doing the same thing himself all these years in Lochdubh? But Jamie had to be wrong about Dorothy befriending Glasgow villains. Maybe he was just jealous of her, like Silas had said Blair was jealous of him. Maybe Dorothy was more popular, better at

her job, happier than Jamie. That could be it—
the green-eyed monster rearing its head again.

Anyway, Jamie and Flora didn't know her like
he did. They didn't have the bond with her that
he did. She would tell him if there were things
in her past that she needed to bury. She wouldn't
keep secrets from him. And yet . . . the day before
the murder he had been sure that she knew
Graham Leslie when they had met in the Tommel
Castle car park. She had denied it. Had she lied
about that? There was only one way to find out:
He would ask her when he got home. She would
have a perfectly sensible explanation, Hamish was
sure of that.

He leaned on the wall and looked out across
the river. The tide was going out, exposing sand-
banks where a colony of seals basked, luxuriating
in the sunshine. Harbour seals, thought Hamish,
just like those at home. That's where I'm heading
now—home and to Dorothy. He opened the car
door and watched a motorcycle roar past on the
main road, prompting thoughts of Keith Bain.
He needed to have another word with Bain, but
that would now have to wait until after the wedding. There was, after all, only tomorrow to get
through before he and Dorothy would be man

and wife. His thoughts now firmly trained on his wedding day, Hamish headed west.

With every mile he put behind him, the hills seemed to grow higher, the trees greener, and the countryside more lush. Eventually, the hills merged into the mountains of the Highlands, and the closer he came to home, the more he began to relax and the easier it became to think. He phoned Fort George, leaving a message for Captain Munro to let him know that he needed to speak to Bain again urgently. He was surprised when the officer called him back just a few minutes later.

"I didn't think you were back in your office until later tomorrow, sir," he said, using the car's hands-free system to talk as he drove.

"I'm not," Munro confirmed. "We're still out here in the mountains, but there's surprisingly good phone reception here, so I'm catching up, keeping abreast of things while we take a break." Hamish could hear the boom of the wind scouring across the microphone on Munro's phone. Clearly the conditions at altitude up in the mountains were not as tranquil as they were on the road. "Is Bain in trouble?"

"I don't think so, sir. I don't believe that he's

been telling me the truth, but I don't see him as a murderer, do you?"

"I wouldn't have thought so, Sergeant. I will tell him to get in touch once we're back at base."

"One more thing, sir. It would be better if Bain talked to me before another officer, DCI Blair, gets hold of him. Blair won't be as understanding as me."

"I read you, Sergeant. Blair has been leaving messages for me. He was next on my list of calls. I'll scrub him until at least Saturday."

It was evening by the time Hamish crossed the bridge to arrive back in Lochdubh. He looked up at the sky, judged the fading light and fluffy clouds to be perfect, and hurried to the station. He had a plan.

"You're back sooner than I expected!" A delighted Dorothy threw her arms round his neck and kissed him. She had changed out of uniform and was wearing a chic black sweater, jeans, and high heels. "Willie has a table for our last evening together before we are husband and wife." She kissed him again. "And I thought we could have a glass of wine before we go."

"That's a grand idea"—Hamish grinned, eyeing the bottle of red and two glasses on the kitchen table—"but not here. Willie can wait a wee while. Get your boots back on and come with me."

With Dorothy in more rugged footwear, he took her hand and they climbed a narrow track up the mountainside, heading away from the loch. Had it been raining, the path would have been more of a burn, but the previous few days had been dry enough to leave pebbles and heather roots crunching under their boots. When the path deteriorated to nothing they scrambled up the steep slope through the heather, then crested a ridge. In a dip before the mountain climbed to its summit lay a perfectly still tarn, a small corrie loch that stretched westwards towards the setting sun.

"It's very pretty." Dorothy paused to catch her breath from their swift ascent. "I never knew it was here."

"I graze my sheep on these slopes in summer," said Hamish. "It's just about my favourite place in all the world. Come down here now—this is just the spot."

He spread his waterproof jacket on the ground, where they sat snuggled together, and he poured two glasses of wine.

"In high summer it gets light here around four in the morning," Hamish explained, "and it doesn't really get dark until near midnight. But at this time of year the sun disappears beyond those mountaintops around now."

As though he had cast a spell, the yellowing sun began to dip behind the distant peaks, the light dimmed slightly, and the surface of the tarn was slowly tinged with pink.

"They call this 'The Ruby Loch' because it's like a wee jewel set in a mountain crown," Hamish said, clinking glasses with Dorothy and sipping wine while they watched the loch slowly turn a deep, ruby red.

"It's so beautiful." Dorothy was curled into Hamish's side, his arm wrapped around her shoulders. "Sitting here with you, this is now my favourite place in all the world, too."

"Dorothy, I need to ask you something."

"Ask away," she said, looking up at him, surprised by his serious tone.

"Graham Leslie—that day in the car park— I thought you recognised him. Did you know him? Did you know him from your time in Glasgow?"

She sat up, placing her glass on a flat boulder,

and let her hands fall into her lap. Her head bowed and she stared silently at the ground.

"We have to be honest with each other, lass," he said gently. "No secrets."

"I knew who he was," she said slowly, then looked up at him and the words burst out of her in a torrent. "I'd seen him around in Glasgow, and when I saw him here I was scared, Hamish. It was like seeing a ghost from the past come back to haunt me. I was terrified all of that nastiness from my time in Glasgow was going to poison the wonderful life we're planning together here. I didn't mean to lie to you, Hamish. Honestly, I didn't. I love you—you know I do—but I was so frightened and I . . ."

"Wheesht now," he said, drawing her close, ashamed to have caused the tears that were now streaming down her face and fearful that they would kindle a few of his own. "I understand. I was told today that the past belongs in the past, so let's leave it at that. I'm sorry I upset you. Let's away back down the brae before it's too dark, and see what Willie has to offer."

CHAPTER EIGHT

Jealousy is when you count someone else's blessings instead of your own.

Anonymous

"That was a damn fine dinner, George. Quite delicious. I think that the best thing any of my constables has ever done is to quit the force and become your chef!" Superintendent Daviot laughed heartily at his own wit and the colonel politely joined in. In truth, he was more than a little vexed that Daviot had worn a light grey suit and a tie that was far too flamboyant for an evening engagement. His own regimental tie and dark suit were far more appropriate, given that this had not been a black-tie dinner.

"You must bring Susan next time, Peter, and

we can make a proper evening of it with the ladies."

"I shall. She was terribly disappointed not to be able to come but it was a little short notice for her. She is kept so busy with her charity work. I think it's a rehearsal for the 'Talented But Homeless Male Voice Choir' tonight. Still, as we had some unpleasantness to discuss, it's better that it was just us chaps, don't you think?"

"Absolutely, Peter. And you won't forget about that little matter, will you?"

"I certainly won't, George. In fact," said Daviot, spotting a familiar figure bumbling up the front steps of the hotel, "our little matter has just shown up. DCI Blair! A word, if you please!"

Blair looked up the stairs to where Daviot stood in the Tommel Castle Hotel doorway, and his face, already slack with drink, sagged even further. The two detectives accompanying him paused at the foot of the stairs.

"Yes, Superintendent, right away, sir." Blair quickened his pace but caught his foot on the top step and stumbled forward bent double, planting his head firmly in Daviot's stomach. The superintendent staggered two steps backwards before recovering his balance with the aid of the colonel's helping hand.

"You are drunk, man!" Daviot roared, straightening his jacket. "This is no state for a senior police officer to be in!"

"Jusht, ummmm . . . relaxshing wi' a couple of the boys, sir." Blair was slurring his words but swiftly recovering his sobriety at a rate that betrayed many years of practice. "Off duty this evening, sir."

"You need to smarten up your act, Chief Inspector." Daviot was rigid with anger. "And not only in terms of your personal conduct. The way you have been handling the investigation here leaves a great deal to be desired. I should not be hearing reports of police officers bullying and intimidating members of the public and the staff of this hotel! Tread lightly from now on, Blair, or I'll have you back in Glasgow faster than you can sink a dram!"

"Wi' respect, sir"—Blair squared his shoulders and now appeared better able to focus on Daviot, although he was swaying slightly—"I didn't ask to come up here to the middle of nowhere. My superiors in Glasgow ordered me up here, and I'll be glad to get out of this dump as soon as our work is finished."

"And when might that be?" Daviot demanded. "There is precious little sign of any progress."

"Most of the team have already gone back." Blair waved a shaky hand in the direction of the two detectives waiting at the foot of the stairs. "Only these two left. We will be interviewing our prime suspect imminin . . . nimminent . . . soon."

"And who is this suspect?"

"A young shoulder . . . soldier, sir. Dodgy alibi. Definitely our man. We'll have him in custody within forty-eight hours."

"Keep me appraised," Daviot barked. "You may report to Glasgow, but this is part of my patch, Blair. Now go and sleep it off—and when you're dealing with anyone around here from now on, you treat them with respect! Do you understand me?"

"Yes, sir. Crystal clear, sir."

Daviot wished the colonel goodnight and marched off to his car. The colonel gave Blair a look of sheer loathing, then beat a strategic retreat to the private quarters. Blair glanced into the hotel past the reception area, then waved his men up the stairs.

"Come away in, lads," he called. "The bar's still

open. I'll be there in just a wee minute. Make mine a double."

Blair wandered into the main hall, rested one shoulder against the bannister on the staircase, and pulled his mobile phone out of his pocket.

"It's me," he grunted furtively, looking left and right to check for eavesdroppers. "Blair, of course—who else? Where are you? Well you shouldn't be! It's not safe. I've got the top brass breathing down my neck. We need to hold back . . . Aye, but the plan's shot to pieces! We need to keep our heids down or we'll all land in the jail! No, you can't . . . ach, bollocks!"

He stared at the phone, the other party clearly having hung up on him, then he wiped his nose on the back of his hand and headed for the bar.

"What was that all about?" Silas stepped out from behind the office door.

"I have no idea." Hamish followed him into the hall, having taken cover in the office with Silas when they spotted the row brewing between Blair and Daviot. "I was told Blair was up to no good, and that confirms it. Whatever the plan is that's been 'shot to pieces,' I'd be willing to bet it involves me in some way."

"Or Dorothy," Silas suggested. "Last night—

before dawn this morning, actually—she had a bust-up with some woman in her room."

"Same woman as came looking for her before?"

"I'd say so. Freddy and me were there pretty quick, but the woman took off in that blue car again. Dorothy told us the woman was her oldest friend but that they fell out years ago. Something to do with a man. She wanted her to come to the wedding, but they argued again."

"She didn't mention anything to me."

"She reckoned you had enough on your mind, I think. She didn't want anything else upsetting you before the wedding. She gave the same story to Elspeth and Priscilla."

"I guess it must be true, then."

"Being consistent doesn't necessarily mean you're telling the truth."

"Aye, you're right." The incident with Leslie the day before his murder sprang into Hamish's mind again. "But it doesn't mean she's lying, either. She's determined to make a fresh start. She doesn't want anything spoiling what we have here in Lochdubh."

"Then it makes sense. Just a bit strange, that's all."

"It is, but it's not half as strange as some of the

other things going on around here. Thanks for taking care of Dorothy, Silas. You and Freddy are grand lads."

"No problem. If I hear anything more on the Blair mystery, I'll let you know."

Having earlier walked with Dorothy from the Italian restaurant to the hotel, Hamish set off on foot to head back through the village on his route home. It had grown dark but he had walked the paths and pavements of the village for most of his life and had no need of a torch to find his way. As he approached the main street, the cottage windows cast pools of light out onto the road and the village's few streetlights illuminated the way along the seawall once he passed the restaurant. He and Dorothy had enjoyed a delicious meal of grilled sea bass, and Willie's glamorous Italian wife, Lucia, had fussed over wedding plans with Dorothy. Shortly after she and Hamish became engaged, Lucia and Willie had offered a very special rate to open their doors to everyone attending the wedding. There would be a buffet of snacks and, weather permitting, they had a patio area for overspill along with a few tables on the street. Given that most of the village was probably going to turn out, it would not be a substantial meal, but Dorothy had wanted to try to include as many people as possible.

The pub was to be hosting everyone for a drink before they invaded the restaurant and Hamish knew that would entail a hefty bill but, once again, Dorothy had insisted that it was the best way to make their wedding an event that would bring the whole village together after the church service. "It's our way of throwing our arms around Lochdubh," was how she had put it. Hamish stood by the seawall and looked from the restaurant to the pub, imagining it all in daylight with the villagers milling between the two. Their quiet wedding was turning into a village festival. He smiled to himself. He and Dorothy had originally planned a far more intimate affair, but everyone in the village had taken her to their hearts and the wedding had grown into a major local celebration. He was happy about that. It made Dorothy happy, so he was happy about it, too. How could he not be? This was, after all, to be the biggest day of his life.

It was then that he heard the aggressive revving of a car engine and a sudden screech of tyres. He turned to see a blaze of headlights

and a car mounting the kerb, heading straight
for him. He half-jumped, half-rolled onto the
wall just as the car's front wing scraped along
the stonework, the squeal and grind of metal
on stone almost drowning out the scream of
the engine. Hamish snatched his hands and
feet away from the car and, unable to check
his momentum, he toppled over the edge of
the wall, falling a few feet to land sideways
in water, which, once he managed to find his
feet, was waist-deep. He howled with rage and
scrambled back up the wall in time to see the
car disappearing towards the bridge and out of
the village. Dripping wet, he dragged his phone
out of his pocket, relieved to see it light up
when he touched the screen.

"Macbeth here, Alex. Get a car out on the
road up to Lochdubh. Some lunatic just tried to
run me down in the village. It's a blue hatchback,
looked like a Ford, registration number . . ."

The noise had brought several villagers to their
front doors and voices called out, asking if he
was hurt.

"I'm all right," he said, waving to them. "Just
soaked to the skin—drookit!"

"What happened, Hamish?"

"Och, some drunken driver tourist." He didn't want to show how angry he was. "Away back inside now. I'm fine."

Squelching in his boots, Hamish trudged off towards the station, muttering to himself. "If that was a drunk driver, then I'm a prize salmon!" He was home and wrapped in a towel, wringing out his clothes, when his phone rang.

"No luck with that car so far, Hamish," Alex reported. "It could have turned off at any number of points between Lochdubh and Strathbane."

"What about the number plate? Whose car is it?"

"No luck there, either. Maybe you got the number wrong."

"I did *not* get the number wrong, Alex!" Hamish growled. "That car nearly flattened me against the seawall. I couldn't see who was driving, but I saw the number plain as day!"

"Aye, aye, I'm sure you did, but that number won't help tell us who was driving it. It's registered to a red-and-white double-decker bus in Edinburgh."

"A what . . . ?"

"You gave me the registration number of an Edinburgh bus. The car had fake plates."

"Fake? Aww, bugger." Hamish groaned. "Okay, Alex, thanks for trying. I'll take it from here."

Hamish poured himself a large dram and sat in a kitchen chair, placing the bottle on the table in front of him, acknowledging that it might take more than one to settle him down and to help him make sense of what had just happened.

A car—a blue car—had just tried to mangle him against a wall. Could it be the blue car belonging to Dorothy's mystery visitor? It seemed like too much of a coincidence for it not to be, but, then again, blue was one of the most common colours for a car after silver and black.

Why would someone want to run him down? Maybe to stop him from finding out who murdered Graham Leslie. That hardly seemed likely. He was really no closer to finding the murderer now than he had been two days ago. Yet the murderer might not know that. What could he have done to make the killer think he was getting close? The only real leads he had followed related to Keith Bain, but his gut instinct told him that Bain was not his man. He was obviously Blair's prime suspect, but that meant nothing.

Who did that leave him with? Bland? Running someone down with a cheap car didn't seem like his style. His alibi for the day of the murder seemed fairly watertight, but maybe it needed closer scrutiny. Bland was a strange character. Hamish didn't feel like he was getting the whole truth from the American, but that didn't make him a murderer—just a pain in the arse.

The most likely scenario was that whoever murdered Leslie and battered Dougie was from Glasgow and was now safely back in the city, doubtless with a dozen witnesses prepared to swear that he had never left. That would mean the car that had tried to run him down had nothing to do with the murder. Could it be something to do with Blair? That seemed more likely, but why would Blair want anyone to run him down? Hamish was in no doubt that Blair hated him enough to want him dead, but he'd want to be miles away with a cast-iron alibi when the deed was done.

Hamish poured himself another drink and finally admitted to himself that the most obvious conclusion was that the car had something to do with Dorothy's visitor and was, therefore, also something to do with the wedding. Somebody didn't want them to be married—somebody who was prepared to maim him to stop the wedding and who had enough criminal nous to be driving around in a car with fake plates. Well, whoever it was, he or she was in for a big disappointment—the wedding was going ahead. He picked up his phone.

"Silas, it's Hamish. Aye, I know it's late. Somebody just tried to park a blue hatchback in my bahookie. No, apart from taking a wee dook in the loch, I'm fine. Aye, that's what I thought, too—too much of a coincidence for it not to be the same car. I need you to make sure Dorothy's all right. Camp outside her room for the rest of the night, but don't let her see you doing that. I don't want her getting frightened."

Wearily, he climbed the stairs to bed, his head buzzing with thoughts about the murder, Blair, Dundee, the blue car, and, most of all, the woman who was to be his wife in less than thirty-six hours. Thankfully, the moment that Lugs and Sonsie made themselves comfortable at the foot of the bed, and way before his head had started to make a dent in the pillow, he was sound asleep.

By the time the sun rose the following morning, a stiff breeze cantering in from the Atlantic had driven the few clouds of the previous evening inland to the east. Hamish squinted at the sky from his bedroom window. The weather would hold fair today, and he prayed that it would stay that way for the wedding tomorrow. Then he shrugged. There was nothing he could do about the weather, and nothing—not even some deranged woman in what was now a badly dented blue car—could make tomorrow anything but the greatest day ever. He hit the shower while Lugs and Sonsie, with nothing but breakfast on their minds, waited patiently at the bathroom door.

Hamish was enjoying his early morning coffee and mulling over what he should tackle first that day when he heard a car pull up outside. From the kitchen, he could see through the open hall door and out of the office window at the front of the house. A black Mercedes. That decided the order of play—Dorothy was first on the agenda.

She appeared at the kitchen door, dressed casually in jeans, a white T-shirt, and short blue jacket, her dark hair tumbling around her shoulders.

"Morning, Sergeant!" she called cheerily, throwing her arms around his neck and kissing him.

"Hope you remembered that the workforce has the day off?"

"Aye, I did." He smiled. "I will just have to do my best to manage without you."

"Well, when you get a chance, I want you to deliver these." She handed him a bundle of envelopes. "It's just a few invitations to make sure that people know everyone is welcome for a drink in the pub and nibbles at the Italian. I know everyone knows about it but . . ."

"You don't want anyone to feel like they're gate-crashing," he finished her sentence for her. "I know, you've told me all this already."

"Good, then there will be no hiccups, and everything will go like clockwork."

"The effort you have put into organising the whole thing," Hamish said, laughing, "it will run like the finest Swiss watch. Now, what are your plans for today?"

"The groom should not see the bride on the eve of the wedding, or even speak to her"—Dorothy waved a finger at Hamish in warning—"so I am off to Strathbane. I have to visit the dressmaker to pick up my dress, then I have a couple of pampering sessions booked at the Strathbane Spa Hotel, followed by dinner and an early night. I will be sound asleep while you and your pals are downing beer and whisky at the Tommel Castle."

"Are you sure you want to do all that on your own? Wouldn't you rather have someone with you?"

"No, Hamish," she said, jabbing a playful finger in his chest, "so don't you go turning up unexpectedly."

"I didn't mean me. Maybe Elspeth? Must you be on your own?"

"I'd rather be on my own. This is *me* time, Hamish. Maybe the last time I will be ..." She caught the anxious look on his face. "What's bothering you?"

"Bland told me about the woman at the hotel the other night." The white lie let Silas and the others off the hook, so that Dorothy wouldn't feel like their friends were spying on her. "Is there a problem?"

"No ..." She drew away from him. "It's not a problem. Just another one of those things from the past that, like you said, need to be left in the past."

"Fair enough," he said, drawing her close again, "but you must let me know if there's ever any-thing from the past that ... well ... might need some help to know its proper place. I'll always be here for you. You know that, don't you?"

"I do." She kissed him and held him tight. "You're the best."

He winced when she squeezed against a bruise he had picked up on the seawall the previous evening.

"Don't worry." He laughed at her look of alarm. "Just a wee bump I picked up dodging a drunk driver on my way home last night. Some tourist who couldn't steer straight." He related the story of the incident on the seawall, leaving out any mention of the blue car, the fake plates, and the determined effort to smear him against the stone-work. Even as he talked, Hamish asked himself if this was the best way to start a marriage—keeping secrets from one another, hiding things, telling lies. Then he looked at her, enchanted by her concerned expression, entranced by her dazzling blue eyes, and overwhelmed by a surge of feeling for her. What did a secret or two matter? What did a lie or two matter? All that really mattered was that they were together.

"Don't go getting yourself into any more scrapes." She sighed, hugging him tight. "I need you fit and healthy for tomorrow."

"I'll be there." He laughed. "Wild horses, or kelpies, or selkies, or . . . no other beast you can think of will keep me away."

"Good. I will be back in Lochdubh at the hotel bright and early. Elspeth and Priscilla are going to help me get ready, and Silas is driving us to the kirk."

"I'd better look out my kilt and . . ."

"No, no, no . . ." She wagged a finger at him with a look of mock scorn. "I am marrying Scotland's most handsome policeman and I want the photographs to prove it. Number one dress uniform, please. You have one tucked away upstairs, don't you?"

"Aye, I do, but . . ."

"No buts. Anyone can get married in a kilt. Dress uniform."

"Aye, okay, if that's what you want." Hamish made a mental note to try on his uniform later that day and check that the silver buttons were still all present and correct.

She kissed him and bounced towards the door, charged with excitement, then paused and captured him with a twinkle in her eye. "I love you."

"And I you, lass. See you at the kirk."

✳ ✳ ✳

Clutching the bundle of invitations, Hamish made his way into the village, strolling along the loch's edge, handing out the envelopes to whomever he met and making tentative enquiries about the blue car. Most had no idea about the events of the previous evening and no one had managed to get a good look at whoever was driving.

Stopping at the seawall, he examined the gash of blue paint below the point where he had gone into the water. He could see nothing that might help him trace the vehicle. He took a look over the wall. The tide was now out, exposing sand, rocks, and pebbles along with clumps of dulse and strands of kelp. He rubbed the bruise on his back and counted himself lucky to have had the water to break his fall. Had the tide been out, he would have picked up a few more lumps and bumps on the rocks below.

He looked out across the loch, hoping to spot a deer or two on the opposite shore. There was none—only conifers swaying gently in the light wind and heather ruffling in waves on the higher slopes. He turned his attention to his own shore, gazing off towards the bridge over the Anstey.

Despite the breeze, it was pleasantly warm in the sunshine, and he was beginning to regret having pulled on his heavy uniform sweater before leaving the station. He would have been better in shirt sleeves, like the man he could now see in the distance, way over near the Italian restaurant. Then he recognised the figure. He was too far away to make out any detail but he could tell it was Blair, and he was talking to someone— a woman, blonde and a good deal shorter than him. He was pointing towards the bridge. She seemed to look towards Hamish, then turned away and hurried off towards a car. A blue car! That was the one—the car that had tried to flatten him last night! He began running, but by the time he had made it as far as Blair, the car had sped off.

"Who was that you were talking to?" he gasped.

"Just . . . just some tourist needing directions." Blair was clearly lying.

"Don't mess me about!" Hamish snarled. "Who was she?"

"I've no idea!" barked Blair. "And you mind how you talk to me, Sergeant! Where were you yesterday?"

"I had the day off."

"There's been a murder, your pal was beaten to a pulp and his house was burned down, and you thought it was a good time to take a holiday? Do you think I'm daft? Where did you go?"

"None of your business."

"I'm making it my business! A wee birdie told me you were in Dundee. What were you doing there?"

"Visiting family."

"Aye, right—more lies. This was to do wi' Keith Bain, wasn't it? You've been meddling in my investigation again! What did you find out down in Dundee?"

"I report to DCI Anderson at Strathbane and . . ."

"Don't give me that—" Just as he raised an arm to point a stubby finger at Hamish, Sonsie popped up on the seawall, reached out a claw, and shredded the sleeve of his shirt. Blair howled and sidestepped away from the wild cat. "Keep that damn thing away from me!"

"And you stay out of my way." Hamish noted with harsh satisfaction a trace of blood on Blair's sleeve where Sonsie's claw had scratched the skin. "The woman in that car tried to maim me last night, and if I find out that you had anything to do with it, it'll not just be Sonsie you have to worry about!"

Blair looked from Hamish to Sonsie, then puffed out his cheeks and turned to head for Tommel Castle, muttering to himself. No sooner had Blair departed than the Currie twins were at Hamish's elbow.

"You were seen last night," Nessie informed him, "staggering home sodden after falling in the loch."

"In the loch." Jessie nodded.

"No doubt once again also sodden with the drink!"

"With the drink!"

"Not me, ladies." Hamish forced a smile, refusing to rise to their bait. "I was as sober as either of you, but the same can't be said of the driver of the car that near ran me over. This is a dangerous person, and I need you to keep a close lookout for the car. It's blue and one of the front wings is now all bashed in. Call me straight away if you see it. We need to stop this maniac driver!"

"Maniac driver!" shrilled Jessie.

"Maniac . . . ?" Nessie looked at her sister appalled, as though she had stolen her line, then they marched off together. Hamish knew he would see them both at the church the following day, possibly at the restaurant, but most certainly never in the pub.

He spotted Archie Maclean sitting in the sunshine by the harbour, looking out over the loch. The oversized denim outfit was clearly not the only purchase Archie had made now that he was enjoying the freedom of loose-fitting fashion. Today he was sporting baggy blue corduroy trousers and a voluminous grey woollen sweater. The sweater, Hamish judged by the pattern, had come from one of a few crofts in the area where local wool was spun into yarn and traditionally styled sweaters could be made to order. He guessed it had probably cost Archie a fair few deliveries of fresh fish. The trousers had almost certainly come mail order. Archie was not one for shopping—the only retail premises he had ever been seen in were Patel's shop for his tobacco and the local pub.

"It's a grand morning, Archie," Hamish greeted the old fisherman.

"You're not wrong there, Hamish," Archie agreed, his eyes fixed on a spot out on the surface of the loch. "Look—we have a visitor. About one hundred and fifty yards out."

Hamish cupped his hands around his eyes to concentrate his vision and stared out over the choppy waters of the loch. A moment later, a dark face with large, sad eyes appeared, staring straight at him.

"A seal." Hamish smiled. "Looks bigger than the ones we normally see in the loch."

"Aye, we see a lot of harbour seals, but yon's a young grey seal. Bigger than a harbour seal. No doubt his whole family's out by the mouth of the loch."

"That's not good news for you, Archie." Hamish lowered his hands and watched the fisherman take a long draw on his cigarette. Having once been a smoker himself, he still found the scent of tobacco sinfully alluring, although he no longer had any real desire to light up. "They'll be stealing the catch from your net while it's still in the water."

"They take a few from the net." Archie nodded and exhaled a great plume of grey smoke. "And off the line as well, but I can't grudge them a few fish."

"Of course not," Hamish smiled. "Gifts for the old souls." Hamish knew perfectly well how many locals believed that people who died could be reborn as seals.

"If I didnae ken you better"—Archie sounded suddenly grouchy—"I might think you were taking the mickey."

"Not me," Hamish said. "Folk can believe what they want to believe—as long as they don't break the law while they're doing it."

"Yon seal could be your man that got himself shot."

"If only he could tell me who did it, Archie."

"He might not be able to, but you ken someone who can."

"What are you talking about? Oh, not mad Angus Macdonald."

"He's helped you afore now, Hamish. He kens things."

"Aye, he knows things." Hamish conjured an image of the self-styled mystic who lived in a cottage on the hillside to the south of Lochdubh. "He may take money for telling fortunes but does as much listening as he does telling. He knows all the gossip."

"The seer kens things that have happened and he kens some things that have yet to happen. He has a powerful gift."

"It's a powerful imagination that old charlatan has, Archie, but you're right. I should have a word with him." He glanced at his watch. "I'll take a run up to his place now."

"There must be an offering."

"Offering . . . aye, he'll be expecting something for his words of wisdom. Thanks, Archie."

Hamish called in at Mr. Patel's shop to find something to take with him for the seer. He had often considered charging Macdonald with fraud for conning people out of hard cash with his bogus fortune-telling, yet if anyone left his cottage with even a crumb of comfort from the old man's ramblings, then why should Hamish deny them that? Besides, Macdonald knew so much about everyone in the area that he could sometimes, albeit unknowingly, supply a snippet of information that helped to link different strands of an investigation. Hamish picked up a Dundee cake and smiled. This was definitely a link—of sorts—to the case. Maybe it would provide inspiration for the seer, and it had a "price reduced" sticker. After paying for the cake, he peeled off the sticker.

The track that led to Macdonald's cottage lay beyond the last of the village houses and meandered along the edge of a small field before rising steeply to where the seer's home perched on a wide, flat, grassy ledge. The thick stone walls were set with small windows and a heavy wooden door with peeling paint that once might have been red. Just as Hamish lifted his hand to knock, the door swung open and the seer stood before him. Since Hamish had last met him, Macdonald had adopted a look akin to that of the kind of guru patronised by rock stars in the 1960s. His long, straggly hair and beard were now almost white and his disturbingly grey eyes focused not on Hamish but on a point that appeared to be a few feet behind him. His small, chubby frame was draped in long white robes, with black beads strung around his neck and simple sandals on his feet. Hamish noted that he had made a couple of concessions to the Scottish climate—thick woollen socks with his sandals and a glimpse, at his ankle, of long thermal underwear.

"Welcome, Macbeth." The practised drama of the seer's greeting made it sound heartily Shakespearean. "Please come ben."

"I brought you something." Hamish held out his offering.

"Aye, that's something," said Macdonald with more than a hint of disdain, his eyes now focusing sharply on the fruit cake. "Something Patel has on special offer." He accepted the gift and led the way into the gloomy room that served as kitchen, living room, and consulting area. They sat in ancient, scruffy leather armchairs on either side of a small peat fire that wafted occasional puffs of sweet grey smoke into the room like Highland incense.

"Ask what you will," Macdonald said sagely, "and I will answer as I can."

"What have you heard about the murder at the petrol station on the road to Scourie?"

Macdonald stared into the fire and held his hands out to warm them. "The spirits are not always clear, my son . . ."

"Don't give me all your blethers. I'm not your son, and the only spirits you're in touch with come in a whisky bottle. What have you heard folk saying about the murder?"

"You would do well to have a little faith." The old man gave Hamish a look of scorn, then appeared to examine him like a plumber staring at some pipework. "You are surrounded by a fertile green aura of growth and love. It glows as bright as the northern lights, yet it is tinged with the grey-green of envy . . . and a dark shadow encroaches. Death walks beside you, Hamish Macbeth."

Hamish felt a cold chill, as though he were caught in a sudden draught of frosty air. He ran a hand through his hair and leaned towards the old man, summoning up as much patience as he could muster.

"Listen, Angus. You know fine I'm not into all this mumbo jumbo, but I need help with this murder case. Anything you've heard might be important. And there's a woman—a small blonde woman in a blue car. Have you heard anything about her?"

"There's no easy answer." Macdonald sighed deeply. "The folk around here may talk about the murder, but they know nothing." Then he looked into the fire once more. "I sense much confusion, great conflicts of emotion. You are mired in a web of jealousy and lies. Only by seeing the truth in front of you can you see the truth beyond. You are at the centre of this, Macbeth. The evil follows in your footsteps just as the son follows the father with a black heart . . ."

"Och, I've heard enough havers for one day." Hamish stood to leave, pointing to the seer's smartphone sitting on a side table. "If you do hear anything, give me a call."

The old man looked up from the fire as Hamish closed the door. A watery tear glinted in the corner of his eye.

"Be strong, Macbeth," he said softly. "The darkness is almost upon you."

CHAPTER NINE

To love or have loved, that is enough. Ask
nothing further. There is no other pearl to
be found in the dark folds of life.
Victor Hugo, *Les Misérables*

"Wait here for us, Stevie." Jimmy Anderson
stepped out of his car outside Lochdubh police
station. "You can give us a lift along to the hotel,
then you can go. I'm staying there tonight for the
wedding tomorrow."

The driver nodded, spread a copy of the *Daily
Record* across the steering wheel, and settled into
his seat. Anderson made for the kitchen door
with a spring in his step, smacking his lips at the
thought of downing a large measure from the
bottle of the Balvenie he had left with Hamish

on his previous visit. He let himself into the kitchen, ignoring Lugs's welcome, and crossed the floor to retrieve the bottle and two glasses from a shelf.

"Aye, go on and help yourself, Jimmy." Hamish barely looked up from the documents he had spread across the kitchen table. "I'm just taking a last wee look at this lot."

"Is that the Leslie file?" Anderson poured two glasses, letting the bottle linger a little longer over his own.

"It is," Hamish confirmed, clinking glasses with a hearty "Slangevar!"

"How did you get on in Dundee?"

"Bain never caught the train there." Hamish shuffled the papers on the table. "His alibi's in tatters, but I'll be talking to him again and we'll get the truth out of him."

"Found something new in yon file, have you?" Anderson drained his glass.

"Not new." Hamish was leafing through the remaining contents of the beige folder. "But something that could be important—aye, here it is sure enough. Do you know who this woman is with Leslie?"

He slapped a photograph down on the table.

Anderson looked it over, pouring himself a refill. He immediately recognised the bald head and mean eyes of Graham Leslie amid a crowd of people celebrating in a glitzy bar. He was standing just behind a woman with blonde hair.

"Don't know her," Anderson admitted. "Looks like a gathering of his Glasgow cronies, so she must be one of them."

"According to this," Hamish said, flipping the photograph over to show some names scrawled on the back, "she is Gabriel Macgregor. And according to this"—he slid a sheet from the report across the table—"she is the head of the Macgregor family in Glasgow."

"But we knew he was connected to that gang. Why is this so special?"

"Because she's not in Glasgow." Hamish laid the picture down on the table and photographed it with his phone. "I think she's here. Not in Lochdubh itself but somewhere nearby, maybe hiding out in a holiday cottage or somesuch."

Hamish hit a speed-dial number on his phone.

"Silas? Aye, we'll be there shortly, don't worry. I just sent you a photograph. Is it the woman you saw at the hotel? Okay. See you in a wee while."

"What's going on, laddie? What's this about a woman at the hotel?" Anderson frowned.

"Not just at the hotel." Hamish sipped his drink. "I saw her earlier today with Blair. They were too far away for me to identify her, but Silas has just confirmed that she has been to the Tommel Castle at least twice—once asking about Dorothy and once arguing with her in the middle of the night."

"You don't think Dorothy had anything to do with the Macgregors, do you?"

"She knew Graham Leslie, Jimmy. Maybe not *knew* him, but recognised him from her time in Glasgow. My cousin's husband, Jamie, told me how these folk can get their hooks into you." A look of alarm spread across his face. "Dorothy might be in danger! We have to go to her, Jimmy! She's at the Strathbane Spa!"

Hamish leapt to his feet but Jimmy waved a hand to calm him, fishing his phone out of his jacket pocket as he did so.

"Calm down now, laddie." He tapped a number into his phone. "There's a quicker way to check she's all right if she's at the Strathie . . . Curly? It's Jimmy . . ."

Jimmy described Dorothy to his contact, then

listened and promised to be on hand for a swift
return call.

"You're not the only one who has friends
in the hotel business." Jimmy smiled, waggling
his phone.

"Curly?" Hamish frowned.

"Curly and me were sergeants together for
years in Strathbane. He's been bald as a snooker
ball since he was in his twenties—that's why we
called him 'Curly.'" Jimmy laughed and shook
his head, sipping his drink and reminiscing. "He
hated yon nickname at first but he soon got used
to it. Now nobody can even remember his real
name and . . ."

"Jimmy! What about Dorothy?"

"Ach, she's fine. Curly's retired now and works at
the Strathie. She's a real charmer, your Dorothy.
Curly says the staff there all love her. She's had a
massage and a facial and all sorts—telling everyone about her wedding tomorrow. Curly says she
had an early dinner and is now in her room. He's
going to take her a 'complimentary' half bottle
of champagne in order to check on her."

Jimmy put his phone on the table and Hamish
sat down again, staring at the phone, clearly still
agitated.

"Listen, laddie," said Jimmy, "and give this a thought or two. Gabriel Macgregor has been seen in Lochdubh and has been seen arguing with Dorothy. She won't want anything to happen to the lassie. If anything did, she would be the prime suspect. She will want Dorothy to stay safe, just like we do."

"That didn't stop Macgregor having a go at me last night." Hamish explained about the incident with the blue car by the seawall. "And when I saw her with Blair this morning, she made off in that same car."

"Blair . . . that scunner will be the death of me." Jimmy's phone buzzed and he snatched it off the table. "Right. Make sure nobody gets near her." He looked at Hamish. "She's safely tucked away in her room. Curly will look after her. Just relax now. She's in good hands at the Strathie."

Hamish began tidying the papers back into the folder, scanning each one, searching for something he was sure would suddenly leap out at him.

"There's something in here." He sighed. "Something that we're missing."

"But we're seeing some progress. We now have Macgregor in the area. That's something new."

"Aye, and she has a driver—an accomplice. It can't be a coincidence that she's here when one of her men gets murdered. We have to count her as a new suspect."

"She could be way ahead of us there. That could be why she tried to splatter you against the seawall."

"Aye, could be . . . but what has it all got to do with Dorothy?"

"They could be putting pressure on her to throw you off the scent. And you saw Macgregor with Blair. Where does he fit in?"

"My guess is that he'd far rather not fit in. When I spoke to his wife, she said he was fair put out to be sent up here—not happy at all. She said he'd been having secretive phone calls, talking to a woman like she was his boss. Could he be on the Macgregor payroll?"

"I wouldn't put it past him."

"That would make sense. He wouldn't want to be here investigating a murder committed by the very person who was lining his pockets. That would bring the whole mess a bit too close to home for his liking. Yet Macgregor would want him to make sure that *she* wasn't under suspicion. Blair could be under pressure from the top brass to crack the case, and from his paymaster not to!"

"Now that thought appeals to me almost as much as this wee dram!" Jimmy gave a gruff laugh and refilled their glasses. "Blair caught between a rock and a hard place. Magic! So where does that leave the young soldier?"

"Blair wants Keith Bain for the murder so that he can wrap it up quickly and bugger off back to Glasgow."

"But Bain *is* hiding something."

"True. He might be a fine soldier but he's a terrible liar. Even if he's not the murderer, he's connected to all this in some way. Otherwise, why bother trying to create an alibi?"

"Well, we'll not be solving any more crimes tonight. Come away now. I've my drinking breeks on and it's time we were up at the hotel."

They climbed into the back of Jimmy's car and his driver headed for Tommel Castle, passing the Italian restaurant on the way.

"Stevie . . . stop the car." Hamish sounded a little bemused. "It's the strangest thing I'm just after seeing, and I'm not believing my own eyes . . ."

Hamish and Jimmy got out of the car and

walked towards the restaurant. In the window, sitting on the table that had become Dorothy's favourite, was a magnificent multi-tiered wedding cake. Anka was reaching up to top the cake with the miniature figures of the bride and groom, both in police uniform, the groom with fiery red hair. Suddenly, she realised that she was being watched and, when she saw who was outside, gave Hamish a look of horror before pulling the curtains closed. Dick hurried out of the front door to greet Hamish with a broad grin.

"Nabbed!" He laughed. "It was meant to be a surprise but you've caught us red-handed! That's our wee present for you and Dorothy. You won't tell her now, will you? She'll love it when she sees it tomorrow. It's plenty big enough, and you'll be able to keep the top layer for the christening cake..."

"Och, hold on a wee minute now..." Hamish held up his hands, smiling and, to Dick's mind, with the hint of a blush colouring his cheeks. "One step at a time, Dick."

"Aye, give the laddie a break." Jimmy laughed. "Don't start saddling him with bairns on his last night of freedom!"

"Well, it's traditional," Dick explained. "The

bottom layer is cut for the wedding guests, the middle layer is sent out to those who couldn't attend, and the top layer is wrapped up and put away for the christening of the first born."

"Haud your wheesht about bairns," Jimmy scolded, "and we'll give you a ride up to the castle with us."

"That'll be grand," said Dick. "I'll get my coat."

Hamish smiled at the way that Dick and Jimmy laughed and joked in the car. Dick had been a clever policeman—a clever man altogether if you judged him on the number of quiz prizes he had won. The police station was crammed with domestic appliances when Dick had lived there with Hamish. Jimmy teased him about all the blenders, deep-fat fryers, and microwave ovens he had acquired and told him it had come as no surprise when he resigned to become a baker. Dick gave as good as he got in a good-natured exchange of banter. This, Hamish thought, was a relationship the pair had never enjoyed when Dick was still a police officer. The truth was, of course, that Dick had never been devoted to the police service in the same way that he was devoted to food. He was a far better baker than he was a policeman. Hamish's mind wandered back to the wonderful wedding cake, then the Dundee cake, Dundee, Keith Bain, and finally the words of old Angus Macdonald. That was when a moment of stark clarity washed over him like a squall of sleet.

Lance Corporal Keith Bain had a lot to answer for.

When they reached the hotel, Jimmy and Dick headed straight for the side room, from which waves of lively conversation were already sweeping into the main bar. Hamish paused for a moment when he spotted James Bland standing at the counter with only a bottle of Coke for company. Bland nodded a greeting.

"You caught your murderer yet, buddy?" Bland asked.

"I think that today I've worked out one part of the puzzle." Hamish joined him at the bar.

"Is it something that rules me out as a suspect?"

"It does not. I am struggling with you, Mr. Bland. You have a good alibi but you're still a bit of a conundrum. I don't think I really know who you are yet."

"I guess I shouldn't have lied to you. It just made you suspicious, made you waste time on me."

"It made me suspicious, right enough. Did it

make me waste time? I don't think so. I know far more about you now than I did a few days ago, and that's no bad thing because I *am* still suspicious and you *are* still a suspect."

"Technically still a suspect—but you know I didn't do it."

"Actually still a suspect—I know nothing of the sort."

"Is an actual suspect allowed to buy you an actual drink?"

"It can be useful to take a drink with a suspect. It might loosen his tongue. He might let his guard down. I might learn something important."

"You might." Bland smiled and signalled to the barman. "But I'm pretty good at keeping my tongue tight and my guard up."

He ordered two malt whiskies and told the barman to put whatever was being drunk in the side bar that evening on his tab.

"That's right generous of you," Hamish said, "but the lads in there have a real thirst on them, especially when they know somebody else is footing the bill. You might want to reconsider."

"No, I've had a good week, and it's only money. What else am I going to spend it on?"

"Whatever makes you happy."

"Enjoying myself with friends makes me happy."

"Are we to be friends now?"

"Yeah, man, once we stop dancing around each other and I persuade you not to be quite so suspicious, I think we will be friends."

Hamish sighed, smiled, and raised his glass to James Bland. "If we are to be friends," he said, "then you must join us in the other bar—but we can't have you paying for everything all night."

"We'll see about that." Bland laughed, slapping Hamish on the shoulder. "It's not the sort of thing for friends to get all hung up on."

They strolled towards the side bar together, watched from the reception area by a disgruntled Blair, who stomped out of the hotel, muttering to himself and heading, as was his evening habit, to the pub.

"Wakey, wakey!" Hamish looked up at the sound of Freddy's voice. The bedroom door opened a little, then thumped into something on the floor.

"What the hell am I doing here?" Jimmy's pale face and bloodshot eyes appeared at the bottom of Hamish's bed.

"Acting like a draught excluder on yon door, I'd say." Hamish laughed. "You look even worse than usual, Jimmy!"

"I've a bed bought and paid for up at the hotel." Jimmy scowled, smacking his lips and running his tongue over his teeth in an attempt to banish the dryness from his mouth.

"You said you wanted a wee walk when we left the bar." Freddy stuck his head round the door. "You sang us a lovely song on the way here. Breakfast, anyone?"

"I'll get my breakfast at the hotel—paid for that as well," Jimmy grumbled, heaving himself upright. Dishevelled, disgruntled, and with the creaking joints of a man who had slept fully clothed on a cold floor all night, Jimmy made his way downstairs.

"It was good of Bland to buy everyone so many drinks last night." Freddy grinned across the table at Hamish, and both men tucked in to huge plates of sausage, bacon, and eggs accompanied by steaming mugs of coffee.

"Aye, and I'd have been feeling far worse for wear this morning if it hadn't been for those pies you laid on. They soaked up a fair amount of the drink."

"Maybe Jimmy should have had a couple more!" Freddy laughed, looking at his watch. "Right— I'm in charge here today, Sergeant Macbeth. We have plenty of time to get ourselves spruced up, dressed, and off to the kirk. Looks like the weather will be fine for the walk."

Hamish showered, shaved, and looked out his dress uniform. He brushed the dark wool tunic, polished the silver buttons and whistle chain, and pressed a knife-edge crease into the trousers. He polished his boots to a parade-ground shine and ironed a crisp, white shirt. When Freddy appeared downstairs, resplendent in a green tweed Argyll jacket along with his green-and-red Ross tartan kilt, they gave each other a nod of approval and set off for the church.

As Hamish and Freddy walked towards the church, villagers who had not already made their way there themselves waved and called cheery greetings. A passing car tooted its horn, the driver waving and smiling. Then Hamish spotted a young man wearing a leather jacket and jeans walking towards them, carrying a crash helmet.

"We've a few minutes to spare, Freddy, have we not?" he asked.

"We do, but just a few."

"I'll be there after a wee word with this lad, then."

"Morning, Sergeant Macbeth. Nice kit." Keith Bain admired Hamish's pristine uniform. "Do all the police around here dress like that?" He smiled to make sure Hamish knew he was joking, hoping for a cheery response.

"It's my wedding day." Hamish gave not a hint of a smile, maintaining a grave expression. "Have you something to say to me?"

"Umm . . . congratulations?"

"I think you know what I mean. How did you get here?"

"Borrowed my pal's bike. Parked it back there by the restaurant."

"So what do you have to say for yourself?"

"Well, Captain Munro said you wanted to speak to me and that I had better be totally honest with you."

"He's a wise man, your captain, but you've not been honest with me so far, have you?"

"No . . ." The lance corporal shuffled his feet, clearly ill at ease. "I'm sorry I lied to you."

"You knew Graham Leslie, didn't you?"

"No, I can't say that I knew him . . ."

"But you knew who he was."

"I did."

"And so do I, Lance Corporal Bain. Leslie was your father, wasn't he?"

"Aye, but I never met him—not while he was alive, anyway."

"Start from the beginning. I want the whole story."

"My mum never told me who my father was all the time I was growing up—just that he was a bad lad from Glasgow. A dealer. He got her hooked. Then, when she got pregnant, he bugged out back to Glasgow. Before she died, she told me his name. I decided to track him down to let him know what a complete shite he was. He wasn't hard to find. A few of my army pals are from Glasgow, and they helped. It only took a couple of phone calls.

"He disappeared before I could get down to Glasgow, but we knew that he drove a yellow Mustang. They're pretty rare in Scotland, so when one of my pals spotted one over in this area, I had to go looking for it."

"And that's when we first met on the road near Kylestrome."

"On the hill." Bain grinned. "You near stood

on my hand when you ran past me lying in the heather."

"Then you got back on your bike and spotted the car at the petrol station."

"Aye . . . rode past your lass in the ditch and caught up with the Mustang at the pumps. He was dead when I got there, I swear it."

"Why set up a fake alibi?"

"I didn't know what would happen when I confronted him. I knew he was a hard man, and if things turned nasty, well . . . I wouldn't have thought twice about killing him after what he did to my mum. I'd a mind to do it, but I didn't. Somebody beat me to it."

"I can tell you that he was not a good man, but you should be thankful to him."

"Are you mental? What for? He never gave me a thought in his whole life."

"Och, but he did, lad. He saved your life—and your mum's. When you had a punch-up with the dealers outside your school, you were a marked man. The dealers and their friends were out to get you, but word spreads fast in their world and they were given a warning from on high. If they laid a finger on you, they were dead men. That came from your father."

"Well, don't expect me to get all gushy about it," Bain snorted. "He owed us at least that."

"Aye, I reckon he did. I'll be needing you to put all this in a formal statement."

"Sure. Anything you need, just give me a call." Bain pulled a scrap of paper from his pocket and handed it to Hamish. "My mobile number. I'll help any way I can. Sorry for messing you about."

Bain strode off to where he had parked his borrowed motorcycle while Hamish and Freddy made their way towards the church.

"The son follows the father with a black heart . . ." Hamish mused.

"What was that?" asked Freddy.

"Something old Angus Macdonald said." Hamish shook his head. "Never mind. Get me to the kirk, Freddy!"

A gaggle of well-wishers clustered outside the dark wooden doors of the church. Hamish smiled and acknowledged their greetings before striding into the church. Inside, the bare white walls made the whole building seem far bigger than it looked from the outside. Tinted light streamed through the stained-glass windows, casting coloured shapes over the congregation filling the simple wooden pews. On the far wall, behind the altar, hung a plain wooden cross. As is the way with Scottish churches, there were no drapes, statues, decorations, or ornamentation of any kind. In front of the altar, dressed in a long black robe and white clerical collar, stood Mr. Wellington, beaming with joy to see his church full and the collection plate ready to be passed round.

Hamish and Freddy made their way up the aisle and there, in the front row, sat a small, neat woman with a blaze of curly red hair.

"Hamish," Freddy whispered, "is that . . .?"

"Aye." Hamish smiled. "Mother is here in the flesh." Mother and son exchanged affectionate smiles and nods without any great expenditure of emotion.

The groom and his best man stood at the head of the aisle while the organist—a music teacher from Strathbane charged with creating a wedding atmosphere without deafening everyone—indulged himself by playing complicated tunes that no one else had ever heard of. All that was now required was the bride, and they waited patiently for her scheduled moment of arrival. And they waited. The moment passed.

"It's the bride's prerogative to be a wee bit late," the reverend reassured Hamish.

They waited some more. Murmurs of impatient conversation drifted around the congregation as "a wee bit late" dragged on a wee bit longer. Everyone was desperate to see the beautiful bride in what was expected to be a stunning dress. Then, when a hubbub erupted from the crowd outside, everyone turned to the church door to see Silas, his Dunbar tartan kilt swinging left and right as he marched up the aisle towards Hamish.

"Hamish," he said softly, his voice strained. "We found this in her room."

He handed Hamish a folded piece of Tommel Castle writing paper. Hamish glanced at it, screwed it into a ball, and dropped it onto the floor before storming out of the church. Freddy retrieved the crumpled paper, folded it out, and read the note, Mr. Wellington peering over his shoulder.

Marry you? You've got to be kidding! You make me sick! Dorothy.

Freddy and Silas hurried after Hamish and were joined at the church door by Jimmy. Hamish was at the seawall, his phone to his ear. They crossed the road and gathered round him. He ended his call and dialled again.

"Dorothy's in trouble! She's not answering. We have to find her! She's out there somewhere all alone!"

"Hamish, she never showed up at the hotel this morning," said Silas. "Elspeth and Priscilla have been out looking for her. They've been all the way to the Strathbane Spa. She checked out of there. There's no sign of her."

"I need to get back to the station." Hamish turned towards home, distraught. "I need to get on the radio. I need to get a search going. I have to . . ."

"Not married yet then, Macbeth?" Blair stood sneering, savouring every instant of Hamish's torment. Hamish roared and threw himself at Blair, but Freddy and Silas grabbed him, holding him back. Jimmy, however, stepped forward and felled Blair with a punch to the face.

"I've waited years to do that." Jimmy rubbed his bruised knuckles.

"If you had anything at all to do with this," Hamish howled at Blair, "you're a dead man!" He ran off towards the station, watched by a small, red-haired woman who was standing at the bus stop waiting for the next bus back to Rogart.

An hour later, Elspeth appeared at the station to find Hamish sitting in the office, staring at the police radio, his phone on the desk in front of him.

"Can I come in?" she said gently. "I heard you sent the others away."

"I need them out searching." Hamish did not look up. "I have to be here in case she comes home, in case she calls."

"Hamish, the note . . ."

"To hell with that note!" Hamish snapped. "Dorothy didn't write that. She didn't abandon me. She wanted to be here, with me! I know she did! I . . ."

The radio crackled with a call coming through.

"Car reported abandoned off the Scourie road. Black Mercedes registration . . ."

"That's it! That's Dorothy's car!" Hamish grabbed his phone and dashed out to his Land Rover. He sped through the village, all four wheels leaving the tarmac when he crossed the bridge and gunned the engine, making for the road to Scourie.

He almost missed the side road. It was little

more than a track, hardly wide enough for two cars to pass, but some way up it he could make out the dark shape and red tail lights of a car's rear end. He hauled on the steering wheel and raced up the narrow road. Dorothy's black Mercedes lay nose-down in the roadside ditch. The driver's door was open. He looked inside. The airbags had activated, blowing dust all over the interior. On the back seat, protected in a clear plastic wrapping, was a white wedding dress. He straightened, standing tall to peer further up the road, then scanned the field beyond the dry-stone wall. That was where he spotted her.

"Dorothy!" Hamish leapt the wall and charged across the grass and mud to where she lay, throwing himself to his knees beside her. She was on her back, her black hair spread around her head on the grass, her face a ghostly white. Her blue eyes stared heavenward but no longer did they rival the stars; their sparkle was extinguished, their life extinct.

"No, lass, no . . ." Hamish cradled her in his arms, then felt a cold, slippery smear on his hand. The back of her head was caked with blood, and on the ground beside her body lay a heavy hammer. Hamish picked it up, stared at it silently, then broke down in tears.

"What have they done to you?" he sobbed. "What have they done to you . . ."

More police cars were now arriving, uniformed officers spilling out, crossing the field towards him.

"She's cold," Hamish groaned. "Someone get her a blanket. She needs a blanket. She's so cold."

One of the officers checked Dorothy's wrist and neck for a pulse and reported to a man in a crumpled suit that there were "no signs of life." Hamish looked up and saw Blair.

"Is that your hammer, Macbeth?" Blair stood at a safe distance, arms folded across his chest, a plaster taped across his nose.

"I have one like it." Hamish spoke quietly, almost as if in a dream. "In my toolbox. In the car." Blair sent one of his detectives to check. The man trotted to the Land Rover, rummaged in the back, then reappeared, shaking his head.

"Hamish Macbeth," Blair barked gleefully, "I am arresting you for the murder of Dorothy McIver. Stick the cuffs on him and get him out of here. I'll caution him down at the station in Strathbane."

* * *

Had anyone ever asked, the custody sergeant at Strathbane Police Station would have said that he had pretty much seen it all—the thieves who swore they were innocent even as the stolen goods were fished out of their pockets; the street fighters who were punching each other's lights out when they were arrested but bosom buddies by the time they reached his desk; the Robin Hood of ale who drove off with a truckload of stolen beer to distribute to the needy; drunks of all sexes in various states of distress and undress; but this really took the biscuit. He'd never seen anything like this before—two senior police detectives trying to strangle each other right in front of his eyes. He sat back and let them get on with it. This show was too good to miss.

"You stupid bastard, Blair!" Jimmy croaked, Blair's hands clamped around his neck.

"I've had it wi' you, Anderson!" Blair gargled, Jimmy's thumbs pressing on his windpipe.

Together they stumbled around the room in a bizarre brawling waltz, crashing into doors and bouncing off walls, grunting, swearing, each growing ever more purple in the face.

"What the devil is going on here?" Super-intendent Daviot walked into the custody suite, barely able to believe his eyes. Blair and Jimmy sprang apart, sucking in great lungfuls of air.

"He's ... got Macbeth ... locked up for ... for murder!" Jimmy gasped.

"Macbeth was caught ..." Blair wheezed, "at the scene, literally red-handed, wi' the murder weapon and a mighty powerful motive."

"Motive? Don't be ridiculous! He was head over heels in love with the lassie. He could never have done that to her!" Jimmy raged.

"It's my understanding," Daviot said, keeping his voice calm, "that Miss McIver left him at the altar."

"No, sir," Jimmy explained. "That's wrong. She just never made it to the kirk. Besides, the pathologist puts the time of death at around seven in the morning. Macbeth couldn't have been out on the road to Scourie then, because he was with me."

"An irrefutable alibi, I'd say." Daviot turned to the custody sergeant. "Release Sergeant Macbeth immediately." He then focused on Blair. "Get out of my sight. Get out of my station. I don't want to see you again until you've caught whoever killed Graham Leslie. Anderson will handle the McIver case."

Jimmy hurried off with the sergeant to where Hamish had been locked up, fearful of what state he might be in after having spent hours alone in a cell. When the door was flung open Hamish was standing straight and tall in the doorway wearing white forensic overalls, his bloodstained uniform having been taken as evidence. He had a look of sombre resolve on his face and dark determination in his hazel eyes.

"Let's get my stuff and get me out of here, Jimmy. I need to be back in Lochdubh. I've things to do."

"Now, Hamish," Jimmy warily counselled his friend as Hamish picked up his phone and other belongings from the desk, "I don't want you going off and doing something daft..."

"My Land Rover must be parked outside. I'm taking it. They don't need it here for evidence or forensics now."

"They've dusted it for prints already anyway." Jimmy stood between Hamish and the door. "You know you can't be involved in this investigation..."

"You can investigate all you like." Hamish

moved Jimmy gently aside. "I'm putting an end to this now."

He drove out of the police car park and took the quickest route out of the city onto the road to Lochdubh. He switched off the police radio and drove through the darkness in silence, brooding and distracted. Even the riotous welcome from Lugs and Sonsie failed to lift his black mood. He fed his pets without uttering a word, then sat at the kitchen table punching a number into his phone, drumming his fingers on the table top while he waited for the call to go through.

"It's Macbeth. I need your help."

CHAPTER TEN

No one in Scotland can escape from the past.
It is everywhere, haunting like a ghost.
                                    Geddes MacGregor

The rumble of a powerful motorcycle engine
echoed up the avenue of rhododendrons and
reverberated off the walls of the Tommel Castle
Hotel, forewarning Mr. Johnson, on duty at
the reception desk, of the visitor's arrival. From
his vantage point he could see through the
open front door out into the car park where
a figure dressed in black leather and wearing a black, full-face helmet drew up at the
foot of the entrance steps, cut the engine, and
dismounted.

"No, no, no, that won't do at all," Mr. Johnson

muttered to himself, striding out from behind the desk. "He can't leave that thing there!"

The motorcyclist removed his helmet while walking up the steps, ruffled his curly hair, and was met by Mr. Johnson at the front door.

"Can I help you, sir?" Mr. Johnson smiled politely.

"I have a message for DCI Blair." The young motorcyclist stared impassively at Mr. Johnson. "My name is Keith Bain. I will be staying at the Mackenzie boardinghouse tonight, room six. Tell him I know who shot Graham Leslie. I saw the whole thing."

Without waiting for a response, he turned, replaced his helmet, and walked slowly back down the steps. He mounted the bike, fired up the engine, and roared off. Mr. Johnson returned to the reception desk, grabbed a notepad, and wrote down exactly what had been said, along with a description of the young man and the number plate of the motorcycle. He rubbed his chin, deep in thought. Blair was a detestable man and he would rather not have to talk to him, but this was surely an important message, possibly the thing that would help catch a murderer. Blair was out, but he had a contact number. He had no choice but to do his duty. He sighed and reached for the phone.

Mrs. Mackenzie's boardinghouse was not in any guide book, was not on any internet listing, and was not recommended to visitors by the local tourist authority, yet it attracted a regular stream of clients passing through Lochdubh. Most were temporary workers—seasonal grouse beaters, forestry workers, or road menders—who would stay for a few days or a few weeks, as long as their contracts lasted. No one ever really looked forward to a repeat visit, yet many did return time after time, the irresistible lure being the rock-bottom room rates. Those who expected nothing more than a small, cold room with a narrow bed and a window that had been painted shut decades before were never disappointed.

Room six was no different from most of the other rooms. There was no TV, the wardrobe was a curtained alcove, there was only a cheap electric heater, and the low-wattage bulb hanging from the ceiling barely yielded enough light to penetrate its chintzy cloth shade. Neither heating nor lighting worked at all unless the meter on the wall was fed with pound coins, which it greedily consumed at an alarming rate. Above the bed was a framed, soft-focus print of Jesus, the colours fading but the bold proverb in black proclaiming that A TRANQUIL HEART GIVES LIFE TO THE FLESH, BUT ENVY MAKES THE BONES ROT.

Pinned to the back of the door was a list of rules, chief among which were that guests must not have visitors in their rooms, must not play loud music, and must be in by ten o'clock at night, at which time the house would be locked up. This coincided with the time when Mrs. Mackenzie switched off the giant TV in her private living room and went to bed. Those who knew the place, however, also knew that the door locks were so old and cheap that they could be opened with almost any key and some would surrender to nothing more than a gentle push. So it was that the door to room six clicked softly open just before midnight. No light crept in from the darkened corridor, but the bulky form of a man slipped stealthily inside, then silently closed the door. In the grey moonlight that fought its way through the grime on the window, the man approached the bed where a figure lay sleeping and slid a heavy metal bar from an inside pocket. Hoisting the bar high in both hands, he brought it swinging down on the sleeping form once, twice, three times, then paused.

The light clicked on. A blizzard of feathers swirled above the bed, the sleeping shape having been composed entirely of pillows and blankets. Hamish stood by the light switch, surveying the scene and shaking his head.

"Crivens," he said calmly. "Mackenzie's going to be fair furious with you, is she not?"

The intruder was now revealed to be a heavy-set man with a round, unshaven face and close-cropped dark hair. He let out a growl of rage and charged across the room, his weapon—now recognisable as a crowbar—raised, ready to strike. Hamish easily dodged the clumsy swipe, allowing the weight of the crowbar to swing his attacker off balance before punching him full in the face, causing him to stumble backwards. The crowbar was raised again, but Hamish now had his own expandable metal police baton in his hand, and he struck viciously at the man's wrist. There was a howl of pain and the man dropped the crowbar, but the force of the blow also wrenched the baton out of Hamish's hand. The man thrust himself forward, catching Hamish with a head-butt to the nose that sent him reeling. Hamish lashed out with his left arm, smashing his forearm into the side of his opponent's head, then put all of his weight behind a right hook that landed square on the man's jaw. The man's legs gave way and he slumped to the floor. Hamish leapt on him and, with practised ease, handcuffed his hands behind his back.

"Who the hell are you?" He rolled the man over. "Are you the one that killed my Dorothy? I'll get the truth out of you . . ."

"Macbeth!" Mrs. Mackenzie stood in the doorway, the curls of her permed hair nestled in a protective net, the rest of her cocooned in a tartan wool dressing gown that reached the floor. "In the name of the wee man! I'll never rent a room to you again! What's going on here?"

Hamish hauled the intruder to his feet and slammed him into the wall, where he stood, swaying unsteadily. His eyes were not focusing and his head sagged forward, as though too heavy even for his substantial neck.

"Rules . . ." Hamish wiped blood from his nose and pointed to the back of the door. "Guests must not have visitors . . . I'm taking him in."

He dragged, carried, and shoved his prisoner downstairs and outside, where the man staggered towards the police station, prodded in the right general direction by Hamish's baton. Outside the station was parked a blue hatchback car with one front wing severely scraped and dented.

"That'll be your motor, is it?" He manhandled the man towards the kitchen door. "Stupid place to park it—right outside my station."

Inside, he bound the handcuffed man into a kitchen chair and grabbed his chin, forcing him to look straight into his eyes.

"Was it you that killed Dorothy? Was it you that battered Dougie?" Hamish let the chin fall when he saw the man's eyes were still glazed and that he could manage no more than a mumble in response. He began rifling through his prisoner's pockets. "Right! Let's see if we can find out who you are..."

"His name is Michael." A slim blonde woman walked in from the front office, pointing a handgun directly at Hamish. "What have you done to him?"

"Well, well." Hamish faced the woman, moving carefully, eyeing the gun uneasily. "Gabriel

Macgregor. I've been wondering when we would meet." He cursed himself for not realising that the car outside had not been left there by the man he now knew as Michael. "He's concussed—probably got a broken wrist, too. He needs to see a doctor."

"He'll survive. Sit there." She nodded to a chair between herself and Michael. "Keep your hands where I can see them." She dragged another chair from the table towards the doorway that led to the front rooms, staying out of Hamish's reach, keeping the gun trained on him, and sat down.

"You killed her, didn't you? You killed Dorothy—or he did." Hamish jerked his head towards Michael.

"She'd totally lost the heid." Macgregor nodded. "She'd gone completely mental. She forgot whose side she was on—forgot she was one of us!"

"She was nothing like you. She was never one of you!"

"Aye, but she was, Macbeth. She was one of us, all right. All her life she was one of us. I picked her up off the street when she was just a bairn—an orphan runaway living rough. She was only ten years old and living on her wits. She was a clever kid and a very bonnie wee lassie. I thought then that we could use her for running errands, delivering packages, that sort of thing. You can send a bairn out with anything—drugs, cash, even a gun—if you wrap it like a birthday present.

"But she was different from the usual guttersnipes. She had a lot more to offer and, oh boy, did she want more for herself. When she saw the kinds of things that other people had—nice clothes, nice houses, nice jewellery—she wanted all of that. I decided to send her to a fancy school for girls in Edinburgh. With a good education and some of the rough edges rubbed off, it was obvious that she would be a real asset, and she was. The other girls at school looked down on her—treated her like scum because she didn't have the right sort of accent—and she hated the lot of them. She saw the things that they had, though—the latest fashions, the best phones, money to burn—and she wanted it all. Within a couple of months, she had adopted their snooty accent and was fleecing the worst of them out of cash right, left, and centre. Blackmail, mainly. None of the silly bitches wanted Mummy and Daddy to find out about the boys they were seeing, the pills they were popping, the skunk they were smoking, or the nose candy they were snorting. She even got me to send her some stuff to keep her new friends on the hook."

"That is not my Dorothy you're talking about. She was nothing like that. It's not the same person."

"You eejit, Macbeth—of course it's the same girl!" She waved the gun slightly but kept it pointed straight at his head. "This was hers. She stole it off a complete bampot in one of our clubs in Glasgow. She's been carrying it around since she was fifteen. A Beretta. Fits nice in a handbag or a pocket and easy for a small hand to hold. Came in handy quite a few times, especially when she started helping to snare some degenerate old pervs for us. We would introduce her to men—businessmen, politicians, even some of your police lot—and she'd lead them on, go with them to a hotel room or a flat arranged by us, then pull this on them before things went too far. That was when we would arrive, show the photographs from hidden cameras, and tell them she was underage. You should have seen their faces . . . After that, they'd do whatever we wanted. She put some very useful people in our pocket."

"You're lying. Dorothy never did anything like that!"

"She did—and she loved it. She was paid well, and that was what mattered most to her. Once she got a bit older, there was no point in wasting her on honeytrap jobs—we could get any tart to do that, and Dorothy was a real smart cookie. I came up with the idea of sending her to police college. That way we could have one of our own on the inside. That worked well for us for a long time. She could get to cops that we would never have been able to reach. She was able to find out who had gambling problems, who was cheating on his wife, who was too much into the drink or drugs, and, best of all, who hated who. Dorothy helped us put the squeeze on more cops than I can remember."

"Including Murdo Macleod?"

"Murdo . . . Murdo was different. Murdo was special. He was my man, Macbeth. We were made for each other. I knew it from the moment I first set eyes on him—and so did he."

"Murdo would never have wanted to live the

life that you do. He couldn't have lived like a criminal."

"You're right. He wanted to get away and to take me with him. His plan was to make some big money fast, so that we could hop on a plane at Glasgow airport and never look back—live the rest of our lives in luxury somewhere in the sunshine. It was all working out so well until you stuck your nose in. You destroyed everything. You got him banged up and he couldn't handle the jail. I tried everything to keep him strong, to keep him going until he got out and we could be together again, but it all got too much for him. The other lags had it in for him. Nutters from other firms and anyone who had a grudge against the cops—and that's pretty much everyone on the inside—made his life hell. He was knifed twice. I bet you never knew anything about that. After the second stabbing they had to remove his spleen, did you know that?"

"I never knew . . ."

"Of course you didn't! Why would you know? Why would you care? You're happy as a pig in shit up here with the teuchters surrounded by sheep and peat bogs. You've got your wee police station. Everything that matters to you is right here in Lochdubh. Well, you took everything that matters to me, Macbeth. You took my Murdo away from me. You ruined Murdo's life, you ruined my life, and I swore I'd get my own back on you. Why should you have everything when I was left with nothing?"

"So that's what this has all been about— jealousy and revenge?"

"Aye, revenge, and when that pillock Blair started sniffing around our territory, he helped me come up with the plan. He knew fine that you only needed one thing to make your sweet wee life up here complete—a woman. A wife. He took one look at lovely Dorothy and knew straight away that you'd never be able to resist her charms. So we decided to pull a few strings and get her sent up here. She was to give you her 'butter wouldn't melt' smile, flutter her eyelashes, and reel you in. She was to get you to the altar and then drop you like a spent match. Leave you standing there in the kirk, humiliated, destroyed."

"She didn't leave that note for me—you did, didn't you?"

"Aye, once I'd been in the hotel a couple of

times it was easy enough to work out how to sneak in and get to her room without being seen. I left the note there. Blair reckoned that would be enough to lay you low, maybe turn you to the drink. Making you a laughing stock would leave you with no friends here, and once you were so demoralised that you were making a mess of your job, it wouldn't take much to get this shitty station shut down."

"Blair's a moron. That plan would never have worked. Folk around here are more loyal than you could ever know... And Dorothy would never have done that to me!"

"Don't be so daft, Macbeth. That is exactly what she came up here to do!"

"But she could never have carried on in the police after something like that..."

"No, but her days as a cop were numbered. Too many other cops suspected that she was working for us. It was time for her to move on. This was to be her last job in the uniform. After this she was to disappear, lie low for a while, maybe change her hair for a new look. Then she would have the chance to make more money than you could ever dream of. All she had to do was to fake it with you until the wedding day."

"You're lying. Dorothy loved me. That was not fake. That was real—I know it was. I could tell when she wasn't telling me the truth, like when she lied about knowing Graham Leslie."

"Bloody Leslie almost fouled up the whole plan. He caused a huge problem with one of our rivals in Glasgow—almost started an all-out war—and he was supposed to be keeping his heid down, staying out of sight until we could sort it all out. Instead, he disappeared, then turned up here in that ridiculous car attracting all sorts of attention."

"So you had him killed?"

"He had become a real liability. It was a right pain in the arse sorting out the mess he left behind in Glasgow. Something had to be done about him, but I wasn't the one who shot him."

"If you didn't kill him, then who did?"

"You haven't got a clue, have you, Macbeth?" Macgregor laughed and once more waved the gun a little. "While you were chasing shadows halfway up a mountain, your charming Dorothy walked up to his car at that filling station and shot him in the heid with this! Then she faked a wee accident to explain why she wasn't where you expected her to be."

"No! Why would she want to kill Leslie?"

"Because she hated him. A couple of years ago he spotted her standing at the bar in one of our clubs. He had no idea who she was at that time and he tried it on with her. She told him to get lost. He turned nasty and some of our security boys stepped in to calm him down. That was when he found out that she was a key player in our organisation. The more he found out about her, how close she was to me and how much she earned, the more he hated her. He didn't see why what he called 'some young tart' should be doing so much better than him after all the years he put in."

"That doesn't explain why Dorothy hated him."

"No, but a couple of nights after the incident in the club, Dorothy was attacked on her way home. She was given a real kicking—ended up with a couple of broken ribs and bruises just about everywhere else. She knew Leslie was behind it and she swore to get even with him."

"That's not true. That's not enough to murder him!"

Hamish sucked in a sharp breath and felt a tear stinging his eye. He raised a hand to wipe it away. Macgregor tensed, shifting back in her seat lest he should make a grab for the gun.

"Easy now." She kept the Beretta levelled at his head. "That's not a tear from Big Hamish, is it? Not feeling such a tough guy now, eh? My, my, this is working out even better than I had hoped, but just you relax now, because you haven't heard the best bit yet."

"I don't want to hear any more of your lies. Why did you take the bait and send your man Michael to deal with Bain if you had nothing to do with Leslie's murder?"

"Och, but they're not lies. You know that. I can tell by that look in your eyes that you know you're hearing the truth. If Bain told anyone that he saw Dorothy shoot Leslie, the trail would quickly have led back to me. Leslie worked for me, there are those who suspected she did as well, and I had been seen with her here in Lochdubh. Bain was a loose end we had to deal with."

"And Dorothy . . . just another loose end?"

"Loose end? Loose cannon more like! When I told Dorothy that she had to come all the way up here to the back of beyond, she thought I was joking. She was a city girl through and through. She liked the bright lights. She loved the nightlife. She hated the idea of leaving all her creature comforts behind to rough it among you mugs."

"So why did she do it, then?"

"Because I promised her a fortune, Macbeth. She'd been to my house in Spain, she'd spent a lot of time in the clubs and bars I own, she'd seen the sort of money that our business brings in and she'd seen how people treat me—with respect. She wanted all of that. She was desperate to have what I had, and I promised her the lot. I would retire and she would be the new Queen Bee."

"I don't believe you. Dorothy loved it here. She was happy with me. She couldn't have fooled me—she couldn't have fooled all the folk around here—for all those months . . ."

"It wasn't supposed to take months, dunderheid! If she'd been in her right mind, she'd have snared you in days."

"She did." Hamish sighed, fighting back another tear.

"Aye, and you her."

"What do you mean?"

"She fell for *you*, you numpty! I couldn't believe it when she told me. At first I thought that was the whole plan ruined and I came up here to try and talk some sense into her but she was having none of it. She'd decided that she was going to have a whole new life here with you. She warned me off—said she would protect you if she had to. That's what gave me the idea. I told her that if she bumped off Leslie, I would leave the two of you in peace. She agreed. Can you believe that? She was prepared to give up everything to be with you. She was even prepared to kill for you! She was in love with you, Macbeth! She was going to go through with the bloody wedding!"

"The wedding dress . . . in the car . . ."

"Aye, exactly—who the hell has a fancy wedding dress made for a wedding she's supposed to duck out of?"

"Why could you not just have left us alone? Why did you have to kill her?" An angry tear streaked down Hamish's face.

"That's better." Macgregor laughed. "Now we're getting to you, eh, Hamish? Hurts when you lose someone you love, doesn't it? She had to die because suddenly the plan that she and Leslie had almost scuppered turned into an absolute diamond. She had gone doolally over this fantasy of love and marriage . . ."

"It was no fantasy. It was real."

"And that just made things perfect! Dorothy couldn't be trusted any more and she knew far too much about our business. There's no way I was ever going to let you two settle down up here. She had to be silenced, and pinning the blame on you would have been the icing on the cake. She dumps you at the altar and you go off the rails and bash her heid in with your hammer. You really should lock that Land Rover of yours, you know. Stealing the hammer from your tool-box was child's play."

"You would never have got away with that."

"That eejit Blair clearly thought we would. He jumped right in to slap the cuffs on you as soon as he got the chance."

"Blair was in on Dorothy's murder?"

"Not at all. He couldn't be trusted with anything important. He knew nothing about it. He counted himself lucky to be on the scene where you were caught with the murder weapon. That fair made his day. I just saw it as another way of twisting the knife—making you suffer, just like I'm doing now."

"Was it you, or was it him?" Hamish nodded over his shoulder towards Michael.

"Michael was driving. We couldn't get to her at the Strathbane Spa but we knew she'd be driving the road to Lochdubh bright and early. We waited, we followed, but she spotted us and tried to lose us, racing off up all sorts of stupid wee roads. But we picked our spot and then ran her off the road. The airbags in her car went off. Ever been in a car when that happens? If the noise of the crash isn't enough to make your head spin, then the noise of the bags going off will. She climbed out of the car looking a bit woozy. She had this in her hand." Macgregor waggled the gun again. "She pointed it at Michael, but I snatched it away from her. She jumped over the wall and tried to run over the field but Michael followed her with your hammer and . . . we left her where you found her.

"Her wee gun will be good for you. Maybe I can make it look like suicide. You know— 'Poor heartbroken Hamish blew his own brains out'—that's what folk will say. 'And he did it with the same gun that killed Graham Leslie. Maybe he shot Leslie too.' That might play well if I put about the story of what Leslie did to Dorothy."

"You'll not get away with this," Hamish warned, immediately aware of how pathetically obvious it sounded that he was stalling for time. "There are others who know about you." He glanced down at Lugs's and Sonsie's food bowls.

"Worried about your wee pets?" Macgregor smiled. "They're fine. They were hungry. I tempted them into the shed outside with a bit of meat and locked them in. They'll not be coming to your rescue."

"Not them but..." There came the distant howl of a police siren.

Macgregor's eyes darted towards the front office and Hamish dived towards her, slapping at the gun. In the enclosed space of the kitchen, the gunshot sounded like a cannon. Hamish felt a searing, red-hot pain and collapsed with blood streaming from his head. He heard a curse, the sound of footsteps, then closed his eyes, waiting for the pain to stop, waiting for the end. But the pain did not stop. Instead, it was joined by dizziness and queasiness, providing an uncomfortable reassurance that he was still alive. His eyes flicked open. He felt warm blood making a sticky mess down the side of his face. He saw Michael, still cuffed, sitting upright in his chair, his head back, his mouth open and a stain of blood spreading across his shirt from the bullet hole in the middle of his chest.

Hamish hauled himself to his feet, leaning on the kitchen table. Macgregor was gone. He put a hand to his head, tenderly feeling the wound where the bullet had torn a furrow that ran from just above his ear to the back of his head. He looked again at Michael. The bullet Macgregor had intended for Hamish's head was instead lodged in Michael's chest. He was dead. Fumbling for his keys, Hamish lurched to the locked steel cabinet where he kept his shotgun. He had the gun over his arm, loading it with cartridges, as he stumbled up the path towards the road. The blue car was gone but there were others, more cars, flashing lights . . . He felt giddy, felt like he was going to throw up.

"Best let me have that, laddie!" Hamish could hear Jimmy. What was Jimmy doing here? He felt the shotgun being wrested from his grasp and then Jimmy's voice again: "That's a nasty leak from your heid there, Hamish."

"Head wounds"—Hamish knew he was speaking but he could hear Dorothy's voice—"bleed

like the devil. Makes them look a lot worse..."
Then he collapsed.

"You!" He heard Jimmy barking orders. "Get
an ambulance here now! You—run and fetch the
doctor!"

"He's already here." Dr. Brodie, the village
doctor, dressed in pyjamas, dressing gown, and
wellington boots, knelt beside Hamish, flipping
open a first-aid kit. "Angela, keep his head steady.
Get some light over here, please! Stay with us,
Hamish. Keep talking to him, Angela, we need
him conscious."

"You've got yourself in a right pickle this time,
Hamish." Angela Brodie cradled Hamish's head
in her lap. "What have you been doing? The
whole village is awake with the police sirens and
the gunshot."

"Macgregor...killed Dorothy...killed Leslie,"
Hamish mumbled.

"Don't you worry about Macgregor, laddie."
Jimmy was still on hand. "We've got her, and
we've got her wee gun. She tried to throw it into
the loch, but it landed on the beach."

"Relax now, Hamish." Dr. Brodie had cleaned
the wound, applied a dressing, and was bandag-
ing it in place. "You're going to be fine."

✲ ✲ ✲

Hamish woke in Braikie hospital later that morning. He knew straight away where he was. There was no mistaking the off-white lighting and the smell of disinfectant. The sheets were crisp and tucked tightly around the mattress, holding him firmly in place. The top part of the bed was raised slightly, allowing him to look out into the room rather than straight at the ceiling when his eyes opened.

"This is getting to be a bad habit." Jimmy folded the newspaper he had been reading and smiled at Hamish. "You wake up and the first face you see is mine!"

"Aye," Hamish croaked. "You're not the prettiest of nurses."

"You've another visitor just arrived." Jimmy handed Hamish a glass of water and nodded towards Keith Bain, who stood at the foot of the bed, clad in a beige camouflage uniform.

"I . . . just wanted to make sure you were okay," Bain said. "You should have let me stay. I could have helped."

"No, son." Hamish sipped the water and cleared his throat. "This was down to me. I had to be the one waiting in that room. That was my job, not yours."

"It might not be his job, laddie, but it is mine," Jimmy complained. "You near got yourself killed. You should have let me know what was going on."

"If I'd told you, we would have had to involve more police in setting up the trap. Blair would have found out," Hamish explained. "It would never have worked. I knew Blair would get a message to Macgregor about young Bain being at Mackenzie's place. If they murdered Leslie, they would want to silence Bain."

"I think you'd better leave us now, Lance Corporal Bain," Jimmy said. "I need to talk to the sergeant alone."

Once Bain had departed, he asked, "So what about Dorothy? Why did Macgregor want her dead?"

"They must have . . . thought she knew something," Hamish lied.

"And she did know something, didn't she? She knew Macgregor and her crew."

"She did. It was Macgregor who visited her at the hotel. She knew them."

"I've been hearing rumours. There's some say

she didn't just know them. Some say she was closer to them than that . . ."

"Jimmy, she came here to get away from all that. She wanted nothing to do with them."

"Aye, I believe that much is true. I'm putting those rumours down to jealousy. It serves no purpose to think of them as anything more than that."

"Jealousy . . . aye, that's about the size of it."

"So Macgregor killed Leslie because he had become a liability. She then thought that Dougie Tennant might have seen what happened and sent her pal Michael to deal with him. They then killed Dorothy because they thought she knew they were behind Leslie's murder. Michael then got justice when Macgregor tried to shoot you."

"That's the way that I see it."

"Aye . . ." Jimmy rubbed bony fingers over his long chin. "But Macgregor says that Dorothy shot Leslie."

"That's rubbish," Hamish lied again. "She was caught with the murder weapon. She shot me with it and she killed Michael with it."

"She says she just wanted to frighten you with the gun. You made a grab for it and it went off, injured you and killed Michael. She says she wasn't anywhere near the Scourie road when Dorothy was killed. She's putting that all down to Michael. In short, she's claiming that she never killed anyone."

"Let Dorothy rest in peace, Jimmy. Macgregor gave me the whole story. She admitted to shooting Leslie. She sent yon Michael to kill Dougie in case he'd seen anything. She was there when they forced Dorothy off the road and she ordered Michael to kill Dorothy. She tried to murder me and killed Michael. Fair enough— the last was a bit of an accident. I will stand up in court—a police officer—and swear to all of that. Macgregor's going to jail for the rest of her days, Jimmy."

Jimmy looked Hamish in the eye and Hamish returned his stare, daring him to challenge any part of the story.

"And jail," Jimmy said eventually, "is exactly where Gabriel Macgregor belongs."

"How come you were there to take my shotgun off me?"

"Your wee vigilante ladies." Jimmy laughed.

"The Currie twins?"

"Aye, the very same. They spotted the blue car

in the village and tried to call you but got no response."

"I was sitting in the dark at Mackenzie's place with my phone switched off."

"They couldn't get you, so they phoned Stevie. Told him there was 'a maniac in a blue car' in Lochdubh. Stevie told me, I knew about the blue car, and we got on the road. We got another call from those Currie sisters when we were en route. They'd spotted the car again outside the station and keeked in from the street. That was when they saw you being held at gunpoint.

"I called in some extra cars and Stevie put his foot down. He can fair handle a car . . . be a dab hand at yon rally racing . . ."

"So by the time I came out with my shotgun, the Currie twins had the whole village out of bed."

"Aye, and the state you were in you were more likely to blow your own foot off than anything else. Doctor Brodie patched you up nicely at the scene, but when we got you here they stitched your scalp back together. They reckon you were lucky. Half an inch to the left and we'd not be having this wee chat. You'll have a strange parting in your hair for a while but you'll not notice the scar once the hair grows around it."

"When can I get out of here? I've Lugs and Sonsie to think of and..."

"Silas is taking care of them, although he's none too fond of yon cat of yours. You get another night's rest and maybe you'll be out tomorrow."

"Good. I want to get back to the station and..."

"Not so fast, laddie. Lochdubh police station is now my crime scene. You'll be taking a wee holiday at the Tommel Castle, courtesy of the colonel. You need to rest. I'll handle everything else."

"It'll take some handling, Jimmy. You're sticking to the story, right? Gabriel Macgregor was behind it all. Dorothy died because we were getting close, okay? We were working for you. It was your investigation. You'll get all the credit, but she was killed because..."

"Take it easy, laddie. She'll come out of this a hero, which she was for standing up to those bastards. She was a grand lass. She was good for you, and I'm so sorry that... well, you know."

Hamish closed his eyes, pretending he was

tired. He heard Jimmy leave, then opened his eyes again. One day, he told himself, when I close my eyes I will see her in the snow on the hillside looking down across the blue water of Lochdubh. Or with a glass of wine watching the world turn red at the Ruby Loch. I'll not see her lying still and cold in a muddy field. Until then, I'll keep my eyes open as long as I can . . .

CHAPTER ELEVEN

'Tis better to have loved and lost
Than never to have loved at all.
            Alfred, Lord Tennyson, *In*
                Memoriam A. H. H.

At the Tommel Castle Hamish was treated as a
VIP, with a wonderful ground-floor room looking out over the garden towards the loch and
the staff showing him every kindness. Silas had
warned him that he was there to rest and that he
must not go wandering off. They aimed to keep
him there—and they would be watching him. For
one night Hamish enjoyed it. For one morning
he endured it. Then he felt like a prisoner.

Pulling on an old bomber jacket that Silas had
brought from the station, he opened his bedroom

window and lowered himself out into the garden. He knew that everyone at the hotel meant well and he didn't want to cause a scene if he was stopped trying to leave by the front door. But he just needed to take a stroll along the waterfront, and then he could sneak back in this way. He skipped quickly into the cover of the rhododendrons, making for the front gate.

"There was I looking for a way to pay you a visit without being seen," came a voice that sounded depressingly familiar, "and now you've come straight to me instead."

Hamish turned to find Blair standing behind him, an ugly, crooked smile on his face. In his right hand was a revolver, levelled straight at Hamish.

"I'm getting fair fed up with folk pointing those things at me," Hamish grumbled.

"Heid's still hurting, then?" Blair eyed the bandage around Hamish's head.

"Hurts all the worse for seeing you. What's this about?"

"Unfinished business. If you testify at Macgregor's trial and she gets put away, I'll be in deep shit with her. Her people will come looking for me and..." He drew a finger across his throat. "I'll end up in the morgue. So it's me or you.

This has to look like you finally let the grief get the better of you and finished the job that Macgregor started."

"Drop it, asshole." Bland had suddenly appeared behind Blair. "Or I swear I'll blow you away right now."

Blair closed his eyes as though praying and slowly raised his hands. Hamish grabbed the revolver before he could let it fall and took a handful of Blair's shirt in his free hand, bunching it up around his throat and pulling the older man towards him. Catching his foot on a root, Blair dropped to the ground but Hamish's hold on him remained firm. Hamish crouched over the quivering Blair, shoving the barrel of the revolver into the side of his face.

"If I pull the trigger now," he breathed, "I'll be doing the world a favour. I promised you that if you had anything to do with what happened at the kirk, I would . . ."

"I didn't!" Blair whimpered. "I told them to let it all go ahead. I tried to stop them. I didn't want to see the lassie get killed."

"Why should I believe a word you say?" Hamish drove the barrel harder into Blair's cheek, breaking the skin.

"Easy, buddy," Bland warned. "You shoot him and it'll be tricky to explain."

"Please, Hamish, leave him be," came the breathless and panicked voice of Mary Blair as she pushed her way through the bushes.

"This part of the garden sure is popular today." Bland shook his head in disbelief.

"What are you doing here, Mary?" Hamish frowned.

"I followed him. I knew he had that gun. I wouldn't have let him hurt you, Hamish. Let him be. He's not much, but I need him. Without him, I'll lose everything."

"Get up, Blair." Hamish sighed, releasing his hold. "The way things stand, I can't really prove that you were on Macgregor's payroll, so apart from this wee scuffle, I can't pin anything on you. I will stand up at her trial and I will testify. I'm sure you'll find some way to smarm your way out of a slit throat . . . But if you ever cross me again, Macgregor's boys will be the least of your worries."

Mary clutched her husband's arm and, head bowed, shoulders drooping, he was led away. Bland let out a low whistle.

"I reckon that was real understanding of you, Sergeant. Real lenient."

"Hand it over." He held out his left hand to Bland, keeping the revolver in his other hand pointed at the ground, but with an easy arm, making it clear it could be brought back into play in an instant.

"Hand what over?"

"Your gun. I've seen enough guns in Lochdubh over the past few days to last me a lifetime, and I'm not having anyone else wandering around my patch with a weapon."

Bland raised both hands from the cover of the rhododendron leaves. There was no gun. In his right hand he held an empty Coke bottle. He pointed the open neck at Hamish.

"Must feel just like a gun when someone shoves it in your back." He grinned.

"You've got to be kidding." Hamish sighed, relaxing his arms. "You came out armed only with a Coke bottle?"

"You came out armed with nothing at all," Bland pointed out.

"I was only taking a stroll. So what were you doing out here?"

"I saw someone lurking in the bushes."

"And you decided to tackle an armed intruder all on your own?"

"I didn't know he was armed."

"You should have told Silas. An intruder is a job for hotel security."

"Silas would have scared him off. I needed to know who he was."

"You 'needed' to know? Who did you think it might be? Why did you *need* to know?"

Bland hesitated for a second, rubbing a hand across his eyebrows as though considering a problem of great significance, then looked Hamish straight in the eye.

"You know I play the markets to make money but I guess you also realise that's not my main line of business. In fact, we're in much the same business, Hamish. I don't wear a uniform or carry a badge—well, not all the time—but we're both in the business of keeping people safe. There are things going on in Scotland that my people are taking a close interest in. Believe me, buddy, we're on the same side. We're the good guys."

"I have no taste for secrecy or cloak-and-dagger games."

"A pity. You'd be good at it."

"I'm happiest doing what I do."

"Can't argue with that, but the way I see it, I just saved your skin and you owe me one."

"I always pay my debts."

"I bet you do." Bland transferred the bottle to his left hand and held his right hand out to Hamish. "So we can be friends. I'm leaving tomorrow, but I'll be back soon enough and I may need a friend I can call on."

"Aye, friends it is." Hamish transferred the revolver to his left hand and shook with Bland. "But if you ever need my help, I'll be wanting to know just what it is you're dragging me into."

"You got it, buddy."

"Right, then I'm off to take a look at my house before the rain starts." Hamish tucked the revolver inside his jacket and strode off towards the village. Bland watched him go.

"Look after yourself, Hamish Macbeth," he said quietly to himself, reaching behind his back to retrieve an automatic pistol from the waistband of his trousers and tuck it out of sight in a pocket.

Hamish wandered down to the waterfront, watching black clouds roll in from the Atlantic and a gathering wind blast white tufts of spray from the crests of waves out on the loch. The weather was closing in swiftly and the late afternoon gloom was fast turning almost as dark as night. There was no one around, the people of Lochdubh having retreated indoors and already drawn their curtains against the impending storm.

With every step that Hamish took, a surge of anger swelled within him, growing like the rising storm. Why had all this happened in *his* beautiful Lochdubh? Why had Leslie shown up in that stupid car? Why did Blair always turn up to blight his life? Why did Murdo have to move down to Glasgow? Why couldn't Macgregor just have left them alone? Why did Dorothy have to die? He marched out along the quay, a few spots of rain turning to a sudden downpour complete with booming thunder and spears of lightning streaking across the sky. At the end of the quay, he pulled the revolver from his jacket and blasted every round into the sky over the loch. Hands working feverishly, slippery in the wet, he broke the gun down and flung its constituent parts far out into the water, roaring in fury at the thunder.

His rage of energy spent, he turned to look back at Lochdubh, the lights of its buildings and cottages spread along the shore. He picked out his police station. The hotel was not for him.

The station was where he lived. Crime scene or not, he was going home.

The storm passed, days and weeks passed, and longer spells of fair weather brought the seasonal throng of summer holidaymakers to the Highlands. It was a busy time for those involved in the tourist trade, but the drier days also meant that other outdoor work could forge ahead. Elspeth Grant had an unexpected meeting with Priscilla Halburton-Smythe at the filling station on the road to Scourie.

"This is a surprise." Priscilla smiled. "I didn't know you were up from Glasgow."

"A flying visit." Elspeth smoothed breeze-blown hair away from her face. "I have a day free and the weather is lovely, so I thought I would drive up to see how he's doing."

"Hamish? He's coping. When he's not on duty, he's here." Priscilla pointed to Dougie Tennant's cottage, where a team of builders was swarming over a skeleton of new roof beams. A tall labourer with unmistakeable red hair was at the front of the building, lifting one end of a wooden beam from a stack. With Hamish at one end and Freddy at the other, they carried the beam through to the rear of the cottage, where it was passed up to the workers on the roof.

"And Dougie is back at his pumps." Elspeth shielded her eyes against the sunshine to look across to the filling station. "Is that Silas with him?"

"It is. I've just brought Freddy and Dougie here and I'll be taking Silas back to the hotel. Dougie's not strong enough to manage all day yet, but he's getting there. Silas has been helping out doing shifts at the pumps."

"So where is Dougie living?"

"At the hotel."

"Really? Expensive—he must have a good insurance company."

"Hamish is footing the bill. He's funding most of this building work, too."

"Wow! That's pretty generous on a police salary."

"One of the things that Dorothy did when she was in Strathbane was to visit a lawyer and make a will. She left everything to Hamish. Quite a bit of money in the bank. The Mercedes was easily repairable, so that's been sold."

"And he's spending it all here?"

"Not all of it. There's a rather lovely marble

headstone and a neat grave up on the hillside looking west over the Ruby Loch. He visits her there most days."

"Oh, Hamish . . . you poor soul." Elspeth choked back a tear. "Do you think he ever loved either of us so much?"

"How should I know?" Priscilla sounded suddenly defensive. "Anyway, it's not some kind of competition. We're not like her. In a couple of days I have to go back to London and you'll be back in Glasgow and . . ."

"Dorothy will still be here. Hamish will never leave his beloved Lochdubh, and she'll be here with him. Come on." Elspeth sighed. "I haven't much time, so let's go say hello."

About the Authors

M. C. Beaton (1936–2019), hailed as the "Queen of Crime" by Canada's *Globe and Mail*, was the author of the *New York Times* and *USA Today* bestselling Agatha Raisin novels—the basis for the hit series on Acorn TV and public television—as well as the Hamish Macbeth series. Born in Scotland, Beaton started her career writing historical romances under several pseudonyms as well as her maiden name, Marion Chesney. Her books have sold more than 22 million copies worldwide.

A long-time friend of M. C. Beaton's, **R. W. Green** has written numerous works of fiction and nonfiction. He lives in Surrey with his family and a black Labrador named Flynn.